RACING HEARTS

RACING HEARTS

•

Jillian Dagg

AVALON BOOKS
NEW YORK

Library of Congress Catalog Card Number:99-90720
ISBN 0-8034-9377-0

Published by Thomas Bouregy & Co., Inc.
401 Lafayette Street, New York, NY 10003

PRINTED IN THE UNITED STATES OF AMERICA
ON ACID-FREE PAPER
BY HADDON CRAFTSMEN, BLOOMSBURG, PENNSYLVANIA

For the Golden Horseshoe Chapter of RWA:
Don't give up!

Chapter One

Kate had expected a small house on a few acres of scrubby land. For that's what her mother had warned her Fitzhenry Farm might be. After all, Arden Fitzhenry, the renegade brother, whom her mother's side of the family had lost track of years ago, had been considered a loser. Instead, Kate peered through the iron gates at the sloping lawns, graced with weeping willows and cherry trees ready to burst into blossom, and saw no loser's home. The glossy black of the gates continued in the trim of the stone house and edged the peaked dormers, roof, windows and doors. There was even a miniature stone gatehouse. And she owned this?

Kate's fingers dug beneath the edge of her white sweatshirt, into the front pocket of her jeans. She tugged out a crumpled business card.

It was a lawyer's card, but on the back was a printed name, *Rafe Colson*, the man she was supposed to meet.

She stepped back from the gates to find a way to alert someone of her presence and noticed a black buzzer on the gatepost. She went over and pressed it, holding it down with her finger. She heard no sound and gave up. Possibly the buzzer didn't work. Stuffing the card back into her pocket, Kate looked through the gates again and saw a man with wavy brown hair walking briskly down the driveway. He wore a black shirt, jeans and a pair of polished tan leather riding boots; the clothes made him appear tall and athletic. As he reached the gates, Kate figured he was probably only a few years older than she was. Angled, clean-shaven features made him extremely handsome.

Kate called out, "Hi. I'm Kate Mortimer, Arden Fitzhenry's niece. I need to see Rafe Colson. The farm manager."

A dark eyebrow rose. "I was expecting you. I'm Rafe. Hang on. The gates are operated from inside the gatehouse."

He spoke cordially but abruptly, and Kate smoothed her golden, breeze-tossed hair from her forehead with a rather nervous hand. For some reason she had expected an older man. This good-looking man made her very aware of her gender.

Rafe disappeared into the small house, and Kate returned to her car. Even though it was a white car, the sun had heated the interior, and she could barely breathe. It wasn't worth turning on the air-conditioning, so she rolled down the window. The gates swung inward. Kate drove up the long, curved driveway to the house and parked in front of stone steps leading up to the black front door with a brass horsehead knocker. She climbed out of the car, closed the door and slipped her car keys into the small purse she carried on her shoulder on a strap.

His boots crunching on the gravel, Rafe Colson strode back to meet her. Kate noticed when he was close enough to look at her that his eyes were a brilliant gray-green color, except they didn't show much emotion. He seemed very wary of her.

"I'm not quite sure how you want to go about viewing the place," he said. "So why don't I show you the horse first, as I have other things to attend to? Then you can look at the house afterward in your own time. How's that?"

"Fine. Whatever is convenient for you," Kate said, thinking Rafe definitely gave her the impression he resented her presence. Possibly he did. He had obviously worked for her uncle. Now he probably had to find another job.

Rafe waved his arm to the left of the house. ‘‘The barn is this way.’’

Rafe’s long stride covered the ground with a purpose, and Kate had to quicken her own steps to follow him. They rounded the house and came upon a beautiful view. A bubbling stream wound through the property, and wooden fences separated the fields. All the trees were touched spring green as if with a paintbrush. Nestled into a hillside was a huge barn, other farm buildings and some sort of a racetrack. Feeling overwhelmed that this could be hers to keep, Kate continued to follow Rafe across the slightly damp grass, a little unsure of what the moisture might do to her new white sneakers. Between the house and the barn there was a brick cottage with a black Jeep parked outside.

‘‘Who lives there?’’ she asked Rafe.

‘‘I do.’’

‘‘Does the cottage belong to the house then?’’

‘‘Yes.’’

‘‘So you lived here as well as worked here?’’

‘‘Yes.’’

‘‘You will have to move?’’

‘‘Definitely I will. Don’t worry, I won’t be here when you move in. If that’s what you’re planning on doing.’’

‘‘I wasn’t worrying about that.’’ Kate bit into her bottom lip. She was worrying more about

Rafe losing his home along with his job. No wonder his attitude seemed cold toward her. Although it wasn't *her* fault her uncle had died. Whoever had inherited the farm, be it her, or someone else, would cause Rafe to lose his position here.

The meadow became a patch of mud, which Kate avoided by walking along one side on soft, dry grass. The barn doors were wedged open, letting in the sunlight. The sweet scent of hay permeated the air as Rafe's boot soles click-clacked on the concrete barn floor as he led Kate past a row of empty stalls. Rafe stopped in front of the only occupied stall, where the name *Talisman* was engraved on a gold strip above the door.

Inside the stall, the horse raised his head at Kate, making her step backward automatically. He was gray, with a broad forehead, a blaze marking, and even in the dim lighting, eyes that seemed to be a silky blue color. He looked right at Kate, and she put out her hand to touch him.

Rafe's hand suddenly circled her wrist. "Careful. He can be temperamental before he gets to know someone."

"Maybe I won't touch him then," she told him, feeling the strength of Rafe's lean body close to hers. She thought she could feel tension emanating from him, and it was seeping inside her, making her very jumpy.

"It's okay. But slowly." Rafe guided Kate's

hand to the horse and let her stroke his forehead with her fingertips. Talisman felt warm and vital, as vital as the man's strong fingers touching her.

Rafe let go of her hand rather abruptly and began unhooking a leather shank from a nail beside the stall, then opened the lower door. "Not used to horses?"

"No," she told him, watching the horse, who was restless and high-spirited on long, eager legs.

Rafe fastened the strap to the halter with a little difficulty. When he had Talisman out of his stall, he walked him around for Kate's inspection.

"You'll see he's in perfect condition." Rafe ran his palm down Talisman's long, limber neck like a salesman showing off his wares.

Talisman certainly looked perfect. His coat was actually a mixture of white and black hairs, complemented by his black mane and tail. His thighs were powerful and his chest deep, reminding Kate of a finely toned human athlete. Only the animal must have been about a thousand pounds heavier.

"What do you think?" Rafe asked.

"He's certainly a lovely horse."

Rafe gently patted the horse's neck, his touch calming thc animal. "He's more than a lovely horse. He's a thoroughbred colt." Rafe pried open the horse's mouth to display a rather devilish toothy grin. ''This registration number confirms his age, which is two years.''

Nervously Kate leaned forward to see a number under Talisman's front lip. ''I see,'' she murmured.

She could tell Rafe knew she didn't really see, and that she honestly didn't have a clue what he was talking about.

''He is a racehorse.'' Rafe addressed her as if she were a halfwit.

''Ah, that accounts for the racetrack on the property.''

''Very observant. Didn't your lawyer tell you he was a racehorse? I mean, that's what Fitz did. He raced horses for a living. I wasn't only his farm manager, I also trained his horses and raced them at the track. At least I did.''

The way he spoke the last few words confirmed to Kate that Rafe wasn't at all pleased about the turn of events that was about to change his lifestyle. ''I didn't know anything about the racing. I was only told I had inherited a farm and a special horse, and that after I had viewed the property, I could decide what to do about it.''

''You will come and live here?''

''I'm not sure. It's certainly an option.''

Rafe's firm, handsome mouth turned down at the corners. ''You can't sell the farm. In this area the land will be bought up by developers for a ski resort. You realize that?''

``I hadn't thought of it that way,'' she said. ``That would be a shame, I admit.''

He let out a deep breath. ``You also have to think of Talisman and the rest of the stock, which I'm boarding out at this moment.''

``There are more horses?''

``Yes. There are more horses.''

Restlessly, Talisman moved forward and raised his front legs. Kate backed away, looking for an escape route. There wasn't one. With adrenaline pumping through her veins, making her dizzy, she watched Rafe struggle to subdue the sprightly animal. Kate found herself transfixed by the pull of Rafe's muscles in his arms and long legs as he brought the animal under control. Rafe's voice was low and seductive, very kind and gentle. He calmed the animal right down, and Rafe looked at her almost triumphantly; his eyes glittered like gems.

``You did well,'' she said. ``He's scary when he's like that.''

``I can handle him,'' Rafe said. ``But not many people can. He's fussy about his handlers. Whatever you decide to do about the farm, you will have to consider Talisman's welfare. He has the pedigree and potential to be a very expensive horse.''

"I won't do anything that harms the animals," Kate promised, but she wasn't sure what her next move was yet. The farm was way more property than she had expected, the house much more luxurious and the horse more important.

She turned away from Rafe, from his brilliant eyes, from the horse, and looked down the barn. It was a place alien to her. Selling the farm would be the easiest solution. She supposed she could sell the horses as well. Then she could stay in her apartment in suburban Buffalo, continue with her job as manager of a mall clothing store, and eventually get over being dumped by Casey a month before their wedding, which was supposed to have been tomorrow.

"Do you want to see the house now?" Rafe asked.

"Please," she told him, grimacing a little at his impatience.

Rafe led Talisman back into his stall, dealt with closing it and began to walk out of the barn. Kate followed. The bright sun made her shade her eyes with her hand, shade the sudden tears. If she didn't remember Casey, she was all right. But whenever she thought about that evening when her fiancé had informed her that their wedding was off, she felt sorry for herself.

Rafe moved up beside her. "Are you all right?" he asked.

Kate blinked rapidly and forced a bright smile. She was so used to faking happiness now that it was becoming second nature.

"I'm fine," she said.

"I thought you seemed upset."

He was tenacious. "No. I'm fine."

"Then why the tears?"

Kate had to admit he seemed genuinely anxious about her. "I was just thinking about something. That's all." She shrugged overtly. "It's okay. Really."

He looked dubious as he tucked his hand into his pocket and lifted out a bunch of keys. He took one off the ring and handed it to Kate. "This is the key to the side door leading into the kitchen."

Kate took the key. The metal was warm from Rafe's pocket. She shifted the key around between her fingers. "Thank you."

"I'm not sure what you plan to do. You can stay overnight in the house if you want. Fitz's housekeepers still come in three times a week to clean."

"Well, I really hadn't considered staying over. I haven't had the deeds signed over to me yet, so it's not mine officially. I was going to drive back to Ellis Corners and then drive from there tomorrow. It's quite a long way home."

"Whatever you want to do. If you're not going

to stay, you can drop the key to the cottage off when you're done.''

''All right,'' she told him. ''I'll do that.''

Kate watched Rafe stride away from her. He was strange. One minute cool, the next concerned. Not that she would have to worry. He'd already told her that by the time she came to live here, if she did, he would be gone.

Kate located the side door of the house, pushed the key into the lock and had to wriggle it around a lot before it opened the door. If she did move here, she would get a new lock installed, that was for sure.

A dark, narrow, tiled hallway led into the kitchen. Expecting it to be old-fashioned, Kate was pleasantly surprised to see gleaming appliances and a scrubbed butcher-block table. Green checked curtains hung from the window and dotted a pattern in the sunshine across the tiled floor.

Intrigued, Kate explored more rooms. They were all vast with inlaid wood floors, thick rugs and high ceilings. Most of the antique furniture was covered with drop sheets. Horse paintings and drawings in elaborate gilt frames hung on the walls of each room. A room full of palm plants and wicker furniture had glass sliding doors leading out to a fenced swimming pool, covered and awaiting the warmer weather. The air was musty, slightly stale, as if someone had left and forgotten to return, yet there was nothing unpleasant about the house. It was beautiful.

The curved oak bannister tempted Kate to slide as she walked up the carpeted stairs; the graceful ambience of the house gave her the feeling she should be wearing a full-skirted dress rather than jeans. Two of the bedrooms had four posters, two were modern. All of the furniture was expensive and well kept. She couldn't understand why her mother's family had such an aversion to Arden Fitzhenry. Or why, suddenly, out of the blue, she had been named in Fitz's will to inherit his farm when she had never known him.

She returned downstairs, thinking if she was getting married as planned, it would have been a wonderful place to live with Casey. Now Kate wondered if this was the place she could come to recover from her heartbreak. Living near Casey in the same neighborhood she had grown up in was quite a strain. She had seen Casey and his new girlfriend, Edwina, out shopping last Saturday. It would be a perfect escape to come out here to live. At first glance, she found the farm too appealing to want to sell it, but she wasn't sure how she would handle living here. She would do what she had decided, return to Ellis Corners for the night. There she would try to make a decision about her future. She definitely needed a future. Right now she saw her future as a brick wall with no gate.

She left the house, locked the kitchen door and walked back across the meadow to return the key to Rafe. He came out of the barn as she approached.

"Did you like the house?" he asked, looking at her with a guarded expression.

"Yes. I loved it. It's a fantastic house."

"It is. What are your plans for the farm, now you've seen it?" He stood in front of her, long lean legs slightly apart, very aggressive. He seemed to be challenging her.

"I'm not quite sure yet. It's a very large inheritance. A lot of responsibility with the big house and the horses."

"You've got that right," he said. "Are you going to stay the night?"

"No. I don't think so. I'll have my lawyer contact you as to my decision."

"I'm only here for another few weeks, then I'm gone. So you have to be quick."

Kate saw that his brilliant eyes were quite cold, and she surmised once more that he didn't like this situation one bit. And who could blame him? He had a perfect setup with the little cottage to live in and this beautiful place to work, with animals he obviously loved. But she couldn't be responsible for his welfare; he was a grown man with his own agenda. If she came to live here, she would hire people to handle the horses. Whether she would race them or not was another matter. She knew even less about horse racing than she did about the animals themselves. But she could always get a job and sell some of the horses.

''Well, I must go,'' she said. ''Thank you, and here's the key.''

He took the key and slipped it into his back pocket, then he shook her outstretched hand. Rafe's handshake was firm and warm. When he released Kate's hand his touch was still evident on her fingers. He was certainly a strong character. She doubted whether she would ever forget him, and that thought rather surprised her.

''It's been a pleasure meeting you, Miss Mortimer.''

''It was a pleasure. Thank you. Goodbye, Mr. Colson.''

He nodded curtly. ''I'll open the gates for you.''

Rafe walked with her around the house and strode down to the gatehouse. Kate unlocked her car door and tossed her purse inside, wondering what seemed wrong. Her car was lopsided. Kate's stomach felt as if it had collapsed into a pit as she walked slowly around the car, expecting the worst. It *was* the worst. Her right front tire was squashed flat into the gravel.

Rafe arrived at her side. "What's going on?"

"My tire's flat. I'll change it." She had never changed a car tire, but she had often watched her older brother work on his cars.

Rafe squatted down to inspect the tire. "Have you ever changed a tire?"

Kate looked down at the top of his head; his thick, wavy, vibrant hair curled at his neck. "No. But I've seen it done."

He looked up and grinned for the first time, and it made him so handsome, she felt bowled over by him.

"I'll change it for you."

"No, Rafe." She called out his name without thinking, and it sounded as if she knew him much better than she did. Feeling suddenly shaky, she said, "I don't want you to do it."

"So, Kate." He imitated the way she had spoken his name as he rose to his feet. "You're planning on hanging around all night trying to change the tire?"

"If I have to. Yes." She purposely walked to the back of the car and opened the trunk. She began to drag out the spare tire. "You're one of those men who think women can't do anything, aren't you?" She dumped the spare beside the flat tire.

He glanced at her. ‘‘No. I’m merely surmising, if you haven’t changed a tire before, you’re not going to be able to change this one.’’

‘‘How do you know what I can do and what I can’t do?’’

‘‘Because I haven’t found your jack or your tire iron yet.’’

‘‘The jack is down the side there.’’ She pointed. ‘‘And what else was it?’’

He moved her garment bag to one side and tugged out a silver four-pronged instrument. He held it up. ‘‘A tire iron.’’

‘‘Oh. Yes.’’

‘‘Got men in your life who usually handle this?’’ Rafe asked, carrying both tools to the tire.

Kate followed him. ‘‘Yes. My dad and my older brother.’’

‘‘That’s fine. There are things men have more strength for. And there are things women do much better than men.’’

At least he gave her some credit, she thought.

Rafe squatted down and removed the hubcap. ‘‘Best thing for you to do now is stay the night in the house. There’s a service station not far away, and in the morning you can take your tire in to be fixed.’’

‘‘It’s okay. I have to go out for a meal anyway. It’s fine.’’

He stood up. ‘‘It’s not fine. This stupid little

spare is only safe for a drive down to the local service station. I don't want you racing around the countryside all night.''

Kate placed her hands on her hips. ''I won't be racing around the countryside *all night*. I'll be booking into the bed and breakfast in Ellis Corners.''

''Nothing wrong with that. The town's quite respectable, and the B&B is a decent place, although it's quite expensive. However, I wouldn't trust this little tire to get you there safely. And if anything happened, I'd be the last person you were with.''

Kate thought Rafe seemed more distressed about what might happen to her than necessary. They stared at one another for a moment, and Kate felt her throat turn dry. He had to be the most alluring man she had ever met.

Finally he lowered his eyes. ''Do as I say, Kate,'' he said. ''I once had a friend who left me one evening, and she lost control of the car when her tire blew. She died.'' He hunkered down again.

Kate's throat would barely open by now. She croaked, ''That's awful.''

Rafe's neck tendons were taut with strain as he worked the nuts off the wheel. ''It happened a few years ago now, and it wasn't on this farm, so this place holds no memories. But I remember looking at her tire and thinking it didn't have enough air in it. When I told her to make sure she put some air in it before she drove too far, she said she would. She promised. I don't think she kept her promise."

"Was she a girlfriend?"

"We dated a few times."

She wasn't sure she should ask the next question, but she did. She couldn't seem to stop herself. "Were you in love with her?" Kate's voice skipped a beat on the word *love*. Love for her was dead.

He placed the nuts into the hubcap and looked up at her. "I don't know, Kate. We were dating. That's all. She wasn't a horse person."

"Is that why you weren't sure if you loved her or not?"

He shrugged. "Possibly. There was part of me she couldn't share because of that lack of interest and knowledge. But we hadn't got as far as love. Anyway." He let out a breath. "I always felt slightly responsible. I trusted her to do what was right, and the moral of the story is, I would prefer it if you would stay the night, Kate. For my peace of mind."

The story told her a lot about him. When he loved, he would want a woman who could share his life in every way—horses and all. She remembered the gentle way he had treated Talisman in the barn.

"Okay, I'll stay. But what will I do about supper?"

"If you don't mind chili, you can share my supper."

"I love chili, but do you have enough?"

He turned back to the car and fitted the jack beneath it. He began to pump the jack, and the car rose. "I always make enough for a few days, some to freeze. I made it this morning."

"That sounds very efficient."

"I'm a bachelor who doesn't like junk food."

"You've never been married?" Her voice also slipped over the word *married,* but she ignored the emotion that welled inside her. She would have to get used to talking and hearing about love and marriage.

"No. I've never been married. What about you? Are *you* married or engaged?"

She drew in a breath, then let it out to calm herself. "No to both questions."

"Career woman?"

"Well, yes. I suppose I am." She didn't have much choice now.

"What do you do?"

"I'm a clothing store manager."

He glanced at her. "Sounds reasonable. You look—fashionable."

She screwed up her nose. ''In jeans and sweatshirt. Sure.''

He shrugged. ''I think you look just fine.''

Oh, *did* he?

''Except it's a bit of a stretch to imagine a boutique manager owning a farm.''

If he wasn't doing her a favor by fixing her tire, Kate would have kicked him for that careless comment. ''Why do people presume that just because a person does one thing, they can't do another?''

''Because you're not a horse person, Kate. That's all. You're obviously a city woman.''

He was right. She had never lived on a farm. She didn't know the first thing about horses, other than that they frightened her. But she would overcome that fear. After all, he had his own fears as well. He was scared to let her leave tonight without a safe vehicle because of the woman who had died. Not that it was his fault his girlfriend hadn't paid attention to his advice. But he did seem to blame himself.

Kate wrapped her arms around her middle as if she were cold, not warm. Despite his disdain of anyone who wasn't a horse lover, he seemed like a caring man, but a man who had learned a lesson and now didn't trust anyone to take his advice. She also thought about their marriage conversation. A few weeks ago, if she had been asked that question, she would have said, *I'm getting married in a few weeks.* Her heart squeezed into a tight little ball of pain. But she swallowed the emotion and tried to breathe freely. All she had to do was survive this weekend. Her uncle had given her an alternative to staying home with her anxiety-ridden family, and he'd given her something else to think about. And Rafe's strong personality and handsome looks took her mind off things as well.

Chapter Two

Rafe jammed the spare into place on the wheel. When the spare was secure, he carried Kate's flat, her hubcap, jack and tire iron to her trunk and packed them neatly away.

"I really appreciate this, Rafe." Kate tugged a rag from the trunk. "Here. Your hands are greasy."

He took the rag and wiped his hands, then holding the tire with the rag, he inspected the tire carefully by rolling it around in his hands. "You picked up a nail somewhere. Here. Look."

Kate glanced at the head of the nail embedded in the rubber tread. She was so close to Rafe, she could smell the fresh-washed aroma of his shirt. For a second there was a tense silence, while she wanted to sink against him and have him comfort her. Rafe was opinionated but that forcefullness actually endeared him to her. He would care, really care. But only if she was a horse person, she reminded herself. Which she wasn't. Kate sighed and stood with her fingers clenched by her side as he stored the tire in the trunk and let the lid fall. She was obviously on the rebound; it would never do to get involved with another man so soon, especially a man who would expect a great deal from a woman. She was sure Rafe was such a man. And she had nothing to give any man right now. Nothing.

Rafe tucked his hand into his pocket and gave Kate the side door key once more. "All the beds are made up. There are towels in the cupboard at the end of the hallway. After all, Kate, you were Fitz's niece. If he was here, he'd expect you to stay. I know that." Rafe observed her with a long look. "I'll see you later for dinner then?"

When he was gone, Kate went to open up the house again. This time the key turned the first time. She chose to spend the night in a modern bedroom with an adjoining bathroom, and she opened the windows to freshen the air. The bed was made up, and she located the towels in the cupboard Rafe had mentioned. Then she went downstairs, out the front door to her car, and carried her garment bag up to the bedroom. She washed her hands, brushed her hair, and changed her T-shirt for a long-sleeved top in a figure-hugging pale blue silky material. She hung a silver chain against the round neckline. Casey had given her that chain. She unclasped it and replaced it with another chain that she had purchased herself.

The air was cooling just a bit as she walked across the meadow to the cottage. Yes. She definitely would like to live here. *Just supposing, Kate, you never get married now,* she thought. *You will need something more than an apartment and a good job.*

On either side of the cottage door were planters filled with purple and yellow velvet pansy faces. Pink and white hyacinths in a flowerbed oozed perfume into the air, a rather feminine contrast to the very male man who lived inside. Rafe had left the cottage door open, and she entered, looking around a room with lots of bookshelves and comfortable leather furniture. A bay window overlooked a tiny garden full of red and yellow tulips. A rosewood table in the alcove of the window was set with ebony place mats. The savory aroma of chili con carne drifted out of the kitchen. She peeked in the doorway.

''Mmmmm,'' Kate said. ''Something smells delicious.''

Rafe glanced at her. He looked freshly showered, his hair damp and curling slightly at his neck. He now wore khaki cotton slacks and a white shirt. "Hi. I didn't hear you come in. I hope you're hungry."

"I'm starving. It seems ages since lunch." Kate watched him stir the chili. "Was this cottage here before the house?"

"Yes. It's the original house on the property. Fitz had it remodeled for his hired help."

Kate leaned against the counter, her hands in her front pockets. "Were you considered his hired help?"

"I thought I was a little more than that." Rafe shrugged, and Kate was sure she saw hurt in his eyes. His voice sounded slightly husky.

"Why do you say that?"

"Because I think Fitz could have left Talisman to me. I was his trainer."

Kate now understood why Rafe was upset with her inheritance. It wasn't leaving the farm so much as the *special* horse. "Did he know how much you wanted Talisman?"

"He knew."

Kate shook her head in dismay. "Then why didn't he leave him to you?"

"Probably because he thought I didn't have the resources to continue racing him." Rafe raised an eyebrow at her. "Horse racing is a very expensive business, especially on the high end. You have to put up thousands of dollars just to enter a top race. I don't have that type of money, but

I would have been willing to take a gamble with Talisman and stretch my limits.''

''Maybe Fitz didn't want you to do that.''

''Possibly not. But do you have the resources?''

''To race horses?''

''Yes. If you keep the farm, won't you continue Fitz's dreams?''

She rose one eyebrow. ''Fitz's dreams?''

Rafe let out a taut breath. ''Kate, I'm not sure you understand the situation. Talisman is on the threshold of what Fitz and I both hoped would be a tremendous career. When you begin training horses, they become like a precious children. You spend hours trotting, lunging and breaking them to the bit and saddle. Then one morning you look out over these fields, and you see the horse's canter has developed into a smooth striding gallop. His body is in perfect conformation. And you know, almost without a doubt, that with careful handling you might have a winner on your hands. Fitz and I have seen that in Talisman. And you would have to see that as well.''

Kate swallowed hard. The emotion in Rafe's voice left a knot in her own chest. She had no idea why her uncle hadn't been more sensitive to Rafe's desires, but she knew, at that moment, she couldn't let him down. ''You think I should continue racing horses from this farm?''

"It would be great if you could."

"I suppose. I had thought I might come and live here, but I wasn't sure about the racing part."

"You have a huge inheritance, Kate. A built-in living racing the horses as well."

She wrinkled her forehead, trying to take in the scope of what Rafe was inferring. "But you said it was expensive."

"If you didn't own the farm, it would be a problem, but Talisman could win a race or two this year and bring you plenty of running capital. There are other good horses who will do you proud as well."

"I know nothing about it, other than I can probably run the business side."

Rafe put a bowl of salad down on the counter. "That's probably all you would need to start with. You'll have to hire staff and a trainer for the horses."

"And pay for them with the horses?"

He nodded. "Yes. That's how it works."

"Will you work with me then?" she asked.

"Are you employing me?"

"Doesn't it make sense, Rafe? You're here now. You have the cottage to live in. You might as well continue. All we're doing is changing ownership of the farm title."

"That's true. But I do have some offers from other farms. I'll have to consider those."

"It's Talisman you want, though, isn't it?" she prodded. If Rafe didn't stay with Talisman, then she wouldn't be able to cope with this place.

"He did figure in my future plans," he said. "But when Fitz died, and I heard about you, I began rearranging my future."

"Now you don't have to rearrange your future."

"Yeah, but different bosses have different ideas."

The idea that she might be his boss made her smile. "All right. Then consider it until I decide exactly what I'm going to do. At least it's another option for you, Rafe."

"I agree. I will think about it, Kate." He began to move dishes around on the counter. "Our meal is ready."

Kate carried in the salad while Rafe brought in the pot of chili. He served the food onto their plates and seated himself opposite her. He passed her a basket of rolls.

She took a crisp, warm roll, broke it in half and spread on butter with a knife. "I have to be honest, I don't know the first thing about horses. Cats are about my limit of experience with animals."

"But you like animals?"

"Yes, I love animals."

"That's a start, I suppose. I still don't understand Fitz's reasoning behind this. He never mentioned he had any family. What's the story on that?''

Kate nibbled some bread. ''It's embarrassing, really. My mother's family disowned him years ago because he didn't live up to their standards, whatever *they* were.'' She shrugged. ''They severed all ties with him and pretended he didn't exist.''

Rafe's lips thinned. ''That was really cruel of them.''

''I know it was. I can't blame my mother because she was just a little girl at the time he married, and she never really knew him. But her brother and sister, who are quite a bit older, just don't even mention his name. My mother hasn't told them about my inheritance yet. She can't figure out where he heard about me.''

''No one kept in touch?''

She shook her head. ''No one.''

''Not even with his wife?''

''No. He married after the problems occurred. What happened to her?''

''Nell died two years ago, when I first came here.''

''Did you know her?''

''Only for a few months.'' Rafe dug his fork into his food. ''But Fitz couldn't stop talking about her, so I feel like I know her well. Her family was from Albany and was wealthy. They dabbled in racehorses, and that's how Nell met Fitz. He worked in their barn. Eventually, Nell and Fitz started Fitzhenry Farm. According to Fitz, it was a match made in heaven. They were so compatible. They both loved horses and shared the same goals."

Kate felt as if she were being told one more time that she was an outsider. Although she wouldn't be when she moved here. She would see to that. "How did Nell die?" she asked.

"Same way as Fitz. She had a heart attack in her sleep. She had been ill for some time. Fitz had also been diagnosed with a bad heart and after Nell died, he wasn't keen on much at all. Except for Talisman. Talisman was giving him a new lease on life. Unfortunately Fitz's heart couldn't go the distance."

"I do wish I had met him." Kate felt anger at her mother's family for their stubbornness and shortsightedness.

Rafe sipped from his iced water glass. "If you didn't know about him, you couldn't meet him, could you?"

"No. That's true." Kate looked out of the window. "But wouldn't it have been neat to have been able to come here and visit him?"

The glass hit the table with a jolt, the ice rattling. "Real neat. Kate, if you are going to take on this place, you're going to have to do what's right for the horses. It's not just playtime.''

She stared at him. ''You think that's the type of person I am?''

''I don't know what type of person you are, Kate.''

''Exactly, Rafe.''

He leaned forward earnestly. ''All I'm telling you is that this is a serious business. Horses are my career.''

''And I'll make it my career as well, Rafe. But I can't say for sure right now because I need to work out some things. I do have savings that I can live on and use for the business. I was . . .'' She lowered her head, and she could feel the tears burning in her eyes once more.

''Was what?'' he asked.

She looked up into his eyes. ''I was saving for my wedding. I was going to be married tomorrow.''

She heard his intake of breath and saw the horrified expression in his face. ''You what?''

''Tomorrow was going to be my wedding day, but my fiancé got cold feet.''

''Oh, Kate,'' he said. ''I am sorry.''

''It happened a month ago, just before the gifts started coming, so I didn't have too many embarrassing moments. I just had to cancel the actual arrangements.''

His head moved back and forth in sympathy. ''What kind of creep would do that to you?''

''The kind of creep who panicked at the thought of tying himself down to one woman. The kind who didn't love me enough, I guess.'' Kate really didn't know why she was telling Rafe about this. Except it seemed easier to talk about Casey and the aborted wedding to a stranger.

''Ah, that's really tough.'' Rafe's hand reached across the table. He covered her fingers with his big warm ones.

Kate wanted to splutter out her tears, but she swallowed them back bravely. She had cried enough. It was time to get over it. ''I think having the farm will help,'' she said.

''It certainly might be a new beginning for you.'' He squeezed her fingers and removed his hand from hers.

She placed her hands in her lap and touched the hand Rafe had squeezed. His touch was electric, and her emotions were a mess. She needed to organize her thoughts and sort herself out. She distracted the conversation from her own problems. ''Things can't have been easy for you lately, either,'' she said. ''With my uncle dying.''

''No. Not easy. I found out one morning when I was doing the horses that he had died in his sleep. I took on the arrangements of the funeral. His funeral was well attended because he had so many friends in the horse world. He was a good man, Kate. Your family has been wrong.''

''I know they have. At least by giving me the farm, he's making them realize that he became a success.''

''Fitz probably had that in mind. He didn't like people to think badly of him. Except for Nell, he lived in the future—the next horse, the next race. He was always full of enthusiasm for everything.''

''I think I would have liked him,'' Kate said.

''Definitely. You would have liked him. I don't know anyone who didn't. Except his family, obviously.''

''I gather they thought he wasn't going to amount to much. My maternal grandfather was a very well-thought-of lawyer. I knew him for a while, but I only remember him as an old man. And I never knew my grandmother. She died not long after she had my mother, who was a late-in-life baby. There was something about not being able to find Fitz at the time his mother died, and I think they just gave up after that.''

''But he must have kept in touch from a distance.''

''Possibly he did, Rafe.''

Rafe smiled. ''It's kind of neat, I guess, that the farm should stay in the family.''

"Then I can't sell the place, can I?" Kate raised an eyebrow.

He looked a bit startled. "I thought you had made up your mind to keep it?"

"More or less. Yes. I don't think my mother's family will be that pleased about the decision, though. They would rather wipe their hands of the whole affair. I think they're embarrassed about it all now."

"I imagine they are. Keep the place, Kate. Make them more embarrassed."

She chuckled. "That's mean."

"Just desserts. And speaking of dessert. I've got apple pie and ice cream. My mother made the pie, not me, so it's quite safe. How does that sound? With coffee?"

"Wonderful. Thank you."

Rafe rose from the table. "We could have it in a more comfortable place? Over there by the fireplace."

"All right," she told him.

Kate carried some used dishes to the kitchen while Rafe prepared the coffee and cut thick slices of pie, which he topped with huge dollops of vanilla ice cream.

"I'd put on weight if I ate your diet," Kate said as she sat in a comfortable chair and ate her pie.

"I doubt it. You would work it off around the farm."

"I suppose I would."

"I'm sure you'll like it here," Rafe said. "It's a free existence. I couldn't live cooped up in the city."

"Have you ever?" she asked.

"No. I was born in Ellis Corners. My parents still live there."

"So you're close to home?"

"Yes. That's why I want to stay here."

He held her gaze with his, and Kate felt rather a tense silence develop. She could hear a clock ticking somewhere. The refrigerator buzzed. She hadn't really thought of it before, but she was completely alone on the farm with Rafe, and for some reason, it didn't scare her, but it certainly raised her heartbeat. Or was it the rebound thing again?

Rafe lowered his eyes. "Well," he said, rising from his chair and beginning to collect their dishes. "I'm going to clear up."

Kate thought his voice sounded harsh in the soft evening. She jumped upright. "I'll help."

When they finished cleaning up the kitchen, it was dark outside and the lights formed a cozy yellow glow inside the little cottage. Kate realized, peering out of the window, that she hadn't left a light on inside the big house, although there were a few outside security lights around the meadow.

"I never left any lights on," she said as she folded a dish towel.

"It's okay. I'll walk you over with a flashlight."

"You don't have to."

He gave her a steady look. "I have to, Kate," he said. "After Jennifer died that way, I see all women home right to the door."

Jennifer. So that was the name of the woman he might have loved if she had been more compatible with horses. "That's fine then," she said.

The evening was quite warm, the air still and without a breeze. Rafe led the way across the meadow to the back door.

"Do you have your key?"

She dug into her pocket for the key and pushed it into the lock. The door wouldn't open. Rafe moved in beside her and handed her the flashlight.

Standing very close to her, he said, "You have to shift the key upward, like this and then turn quickly." The door swung open.

"Maybe it needs a new lock," Kate remarked.

"Possibly. I'll go first with the flashlight. Give it to me."

She handed it to him. Their fingers brushed.

"Why don't you get up early and come out to see Talisman's exercise regime?" he suggested.

"That would be fun," she said. "I'll do that."

"Great." Rafe shifted the flashlight in his hand. "I'll go and turn on the kitchen light for you."

When the light was on, Kate joined him in the kitchen.

He clicked the flashlight on and off. "I'll see you tomorrow morning?"

"Yes, you will," she promised.

"Goodnight, Kate."

"Goodnight, Rafe. Thank you very much for dinner."

He turned away into the hallway, and she heard the door close quietly behind him. Then for a second she closed her eyes and told herself to get a grip. What did she expect him to do? Kiss her? The last thing she needed was kisses from a strange man. That was certainly no way to get over Casey. It would just tumble her headfirst into more emotional chaos.

She rubbed a slight headache on her forehead. Tonight was supposed to have been her wedding rehearsal. Strange, that when she was with Rafe, she had forgotten about it.

Still, Kate knew she wouldn't be able to fall asleep yet, so she explored the house. Instead of wondering about Rafe or her non-wedding day, she kept her mind focused on the problem her unknown uncle had posed her. She ended up in what was probably her uncle's study and sank down into the creaky leather desk chair. She swung around in the chair, feeling most executive at the big desk. Her nostrils quivered over the leathery smell of the room. It was a real honest to goodness study, she decided. Most of the walls were bookshelves. Some of the shelves were used to display racing trophies, some for books. She got up to look at the trophies. Among them were framed photographs of someone she thought was Uncle Fitz. He had thick white hair and a grizzled, tanned face. In one photograph he held a trophy high in the air, and he looked so triumphant, so proud. In another photograph he was turned in profile toward a horse, and his face was gentle as he observed the animal.

Feeling as if she had been drawn into another world, Kate went on to peruse the book titles. They were all horse books, and she selected some from the shelves to take up to bed to read. She might as well learn a little more. Then when she met Rafe outside in the early morning to see Talisman, she would appear more knowledgeable. She was going to have to know more anyway if she was going to be Talisman's owner.

Did that mean she had made up her mind to keep the house, move here and actually race horses for a living? She still wasn't sure, but she was on her way to becoming a little more certain. Anything to get away from the depths of despair she had been living in since Casey had dumped her. Nevertheless, she knew she wouldn't be able to do it without Rafe staying on to help her.

Chapter Three

Clanking and scraping noises outside made Kate jump from the bed and dash to the window. Through dull morning light she saw Rafe in jeans and a thick black sweater carrying a pail of water. She ran and picked up her watch off the bedside table. She had slept way later than she had intended, slept better than she had ever thought possible on the eve of her wedding. Burying the hurt that sat above her like a cloud and was never going to go away, she looked at the books in a pile on the floor. She had read so late, she had fallen asleep with a book in her hands.

Quickly Kate shed her cotton nightshirt and slipped into her jeans, a navy blue sweatshirt, socks and her sneakers. She brushed her hair and dampened her face with a warm cloth, hoping to wake herself up.

Kate rushed downstairs and out of the house by the side door. She left it ajar, so she wouldn't have to struggle with the key later and ran across the soaking grass, feeling the moisture seep into her sneakers to make her socks squishy. She found Rafe pitchforking hay. She was out of breath, her heart hammering in her ears. "Hi. Sorry I'm late."

He didn't look at her. "You're not late. I really didn't expect you."

Rafe tossed hay with the fork, his movements swift and sure, his muscular body moving economically.

"I overslept. I don't have an alarm clock with me."

He stopped pitching, propped the fork in the hay and leaned on the handle, his gray-green gaze locking with her blue ones. "You know, Kate, if you have horses to care for, just saying you'll be here to look after them won't keep them alive. Horses are a full-time, day-and-night exercise."

"I'll have an alarm clock when I live here. Besides, I'm going to hire someone to look after the horses, aren't I?" Kate stuck her hands into her back pockets. "You're the first to apply for the job. Have you made a decision yet?"

Rafe looked at the serene landscape. "Well, I've thought about it overnight. And I would certainly cherish the opportunity to stay here and work. But . . ." He shook his head. "It's a huge undertaking, Kate. And you don't know much about horses, do you?"

She gritted her teeth, so she wouldn't explode at him. "I imagine lots of people who have racehorses for investments don't know much about the business. They probably learned, as I intend to learn."

"That's true, I suppose."

"I'm a quick learner," she added. "Please, Rafe. You've been training Talisman. You might as well continue. Why not?" If Rafe didn't take her offer, then she might sell the farm. She would have to make sure the person who took over would love the horses, though. Uncle Fitz had entrusted her with his animals, and she kept seeing Uncle Fitz's white-haired image from his photographs, as if he were overseeing her decisions.

"If you want the truth, it's because we'll be boss and employee."

Kate took a step back from him and inclined her head to one side. He had mentioned something like this before. She smiled with mock sweetness. "And you don't like a woman boss? Or don't like me in particular?"

"It's nothing to do with liking or not liking you. It's not personal."

"Then what is it, Rafe?"

He withdrew the fork from the hay. "I just believe this has to be thought out in some detail. We can't rush into anything."

"I thought you wanted to stay here and train Talisman. Isn't that what you've been hinting to me? Aren't your dreams tied up in him, like my uncle's were? Isn't that what you said last night?"

"I admit that."

"But you were okay with my uncle as a boss, but not me?"

His silence said it all to Kate. She looked up at the morning sky with exasperation. She needed an answer and she had one. At least she had another idea. "Okay. If you want, you can put some money into the horse side of the business. If that will make you feel better. Then I won't be your boss, I'll be your partner. Financially, that will be better for me as well."

"I could do that," he agreed. "As a matter of fact, that's a good idea, Kate."

She tapped her forehead. "There is something inside here other than female mush, Rafe."

He gave her a little smile. "I'm not doubting your abilities, Kate. But I would like more time to think it over. I'll have to see how much I have to invest."

"I realize there are things to work out. I'll go home and make the arrangements. I'll contact you on Monday afternoon, or Tuesday at the latest to let you know.'' She dug into her pocket and tugged out the now completely creased lawyer's card. ''This is the lawyer I was dealing with, and he knows Fitz's lawyer. You can tell him how much you can invest, so he has some idea of how to divide the assets. All right? And then we'll have to sign some papers or something to make it legal. You might have to come into the city.''

Rafe inclined his head as he took the card from her. ''That's okay. Do you have my phone number?''

''No.''

''Before you leave, you'll have to stop by the cottage to return the key. You can have some breakfast, and I'll give you my number.''

''Thank you,'' she told him, actually feeling as if she had broken down a door and had moved closer to him. She didn't know why she trusted him so fully to consider going into business with him. She just did. And she was sure her instincts were right.

Kate returned to the house to prepare to leave the farm. When she was ready, she carried her luggage down to her car, remembering she had a flat tire to deal with before she went any distance today. She had forgotten about that problem. When she went for breakfast, she would ask Rafe where to get the tire fixed.

Kate walked over to the cottage with a spring to her step, which she knew she had never thought possible a few days ago. This was supposed to have been her wedding day and it wasn't. But she loved projects and she had a new one, a challenging one. She had grown tired of her job, and the thought of beginning a new career, which would be her own business, was thrilling. Rafe had left the cottage door ajar, so she went inside.

He came out of the kitchen, and she put the house key down on the table. "Thank you for letting me stay in the house."

"It worked out fine. While you eat breakfast, I'll arrange an appointment for that tire."

He led Kate into the kitchen, and she perched on a stool at the island. Rafe served her a large glass of orange juice and a mug of coffee. A plate, butter and strawberry preserve were beside her. Rafe soon added two slices of toast to her plate. He was really very domestic. She liked that about him.

"You've been kind to feed me," she said.

One dark eyebrow rose. "And if I didn't?"

"I would have starved." *Of loneliness and everything else*, she thought as their eyes met. It was Rafe who glanced away first. Kate saw him let out a deep breath.

"I'll go phone now," he said and strode into the other room, where the phone was.

Kate finished her toast and coffee, and rinsed her dishes and her hands at the sink. As she walked out into the other room, Rafe put down the receiver. "It's taken care of."

Rafe drew her a map, showing her the location of the garage. He told her to see Phil Green. Then he wrote down his own phone number.

Kate folded the piece of paper with the thick black handwriting and drawings upon it. "Thank you very much."

Rafe walked silently with her to her car and closed the door for her when she was fastened into her seatbelt. He was safety-conscious, she realized. She rolled down the window.

"Okay?" he asked.

"I think so." She had the feeling he was asking about her emotional state.

"One day," he said softly. "You might come to realize that you weren't meant for the guy."

So he *was* thinking about her wedding day. "Maybe one day," she agreed. "But not today. Not yet. I had a beautiful dress. Long, white. Beautiful."

He smiled sadly and straightened. "I'll go open the gate for you."

With Rafe's map, Kate found the small service station quite easily. Leaving her car parked outside, she walked into the oily-smelling office and asked for Phil Green. The young man in jeans and shirt smiled at her.

"I'm Phil. Are you Kate? Rafe said you were a pretty blonde."

That Rafe had actually told someone he thought she was pretty made Kate feel unexpectedly warm inside.

"Is it a tire problem?" Phil asked.

Kate nodded. "Yes. Rafe put the spare on for me last night. There's a nail in the tire."

"Known him long?" Phil asked as he opened her trunk and took out her tire.

"I just met him. My uncle was Arden Fitzhenry."

Phil's eyes rounded. "Oh. Well. You're the one who inherited the farm?"

"Yes. Rafe tell you?"

"He mentioned Fitz had left the farm to a niece or something like that. He was pretty steamed up about a horse. I guess it's a pretty valuable horse with some pedigree."

Kate leaned on the car as Phil rotated the tire to find the nail. "You know horses then?"

"My dad breeds them. This was my grandad's business. I service all the farm vehicles around here." He found the nail. "Ah. There it is. This won't take long. Do you want some coffee or a soda pop or juice?"

"Juice sounds good," she said, following Phil back into the greasy office.

He selected a bottle of ruby red tropical juice from the cooler and handed it to her. "This is tasty stuff. I'll just go and fix the tire and put it back on your car. Relax."

Kate paced, sipping from her drink. How could she relax when she was the new owner of a horse farm?

She considered her new future all the way home, and she was excited by the time she reached the city limits. *This is so different from Fitzhenry Farm,* she thought as she drove through suburbs and turned into the private parking lot of her high-rise apartment block.

Kate's brother Joe's blue mini-van was in the visitor parking spot. She carried her garment bag and purse to the front door and found him sitting in the sunshine on the brick flower planter with his wife, Kim. Kim jumped up when she saw her sister-in-law. She was tall, her hair a lush dark brown bell around her head. She was dressed in the same style as her husband, sweatshirt and jeans. "Where have you been, Katie? We were *so* worried about you."

Everyone in her family had been watching her like hawks since Casey had walked out on her.

"Yeah, where have you been, Katie?" Joe drawled, tucking his arm around his wife's waist and giving his sister a stare, his blue eyes very similar to her own. Joe had fair, straight sandy hair and a muscular body that he kept fit with football and weight lifting. He was two years older than Kate and had always been very protective of her.

"Where have I been?" she asked mysteriously, letting her family members into the front door of her apartment building. They stood in the marble-floored foyer near the elevator. "I went to Fitzhenry Farm."

"We should have thought of that," Joe said with a sigh. "We were all trying to phone you last evening, and when there was no answer we began to get frantic. That's why we're here waiting today."

The elevator doors opened and they all got on. Kate pushed the button to the tenth floor. "I thought I would take the opportunity yesterday to go, to get away, you know."

"I agree," Kim said softly. "Are you okay?"

"I'm not bad. You should see the horse farm I've inherited. It's fantastic."

"It's not a hovel?" Joe asked.

"No. It's not a hovel. Mother's all wrong about Uncle Fitz. He was a successful racehorse owner. I intend to keep the horses and race them. That's what I'll do for a living." Her plans sounded so real when she spoke them aloud like that.

Her brother's eyes opened wide. "You mean you'll move out there and give up your job?"

"Yes, Joe. That's what I'm saying."

They reached the tenth floor. Kate went ahead and opened the door into her apartment. It was a big apartment, with two bedrooms, a kitchen and two bathrooms. The living-room windows faced out over a park with lots of trees. It was a neat, clean living space, but she didn't have much feeling for it, especially because it held memories of dating Casey. She certainly wouldn't be sorry to pack her few things and move into Fitzhenry Farm. No, not sorry at all.

"Do you want coffee or something cold to drink?" Kate asked, dumping her garment bag down onto the carpet.

"Milk for me," Kim said. "Joe will probably have a beer."

"I'll get it," Joe said. "What do you want, Kate?"

"Open a can of pop for me, Joe. That's fine. Sit down, Kim, and I'll explain everything."

By the time Kate got through explaining the situation she had found at Fitzhenry Farm, the other two were staring at her.

"Let me get this straight," her brother said, holding his hand in the air. He counted off one finger. ''First you're going to move into Fitzhenry Farm?''

Kate nodded. ''Yes.''

He bent another finger. ''Second, you're considering going into a business partnership with a man you only met at Fitz's house. A dubious sort I would say, if he's into horse racing.''

''He is not dubious, Joe. He's perfectly on the level. He was Uncle's trainer and managed the farm for him.''

Joe marked off another finger. ''And that brings us to three, Kate. Uncle Fitz, from all accounts, wasn't fit to be in the family.''

''You wait until you see his house, Joe. You won't think that. The man was wealthy.'' Kate got up. ''Anyway, I don't want to hear all this negativity. I only want to be positive. I'm doing it. I'm going to make it work.''

''Number four,'' Joe said, ignoring her. ''You're not doing this just because of Casey. Not some kind of rebound-stupid thing.''

''No. I'm not. Okay, maybe a little, Joe, but I have to do something. I was supposed to be in Cancún on my honeymoon tonight, and where am I? Home alone. I didn't ask Uncle Fitz to leave me his farm, but he did, and it's perfect timing, when I need to make changes in my life. I probably will never get married now, so I have to do something with my life.''

‘‘You’ll get married, Kate,’’ Kim put in.

‘‘I don’t think so. I’ve been hurt enough. I feel exhausted from the hurt. I just want to live contentedly.’’

‘‘But being married is so much fun,’’ Joe said.

‘‘Maybe for you, but Casey couldn’t see that, could he? Now I don’t want to talk about him. He’s over.’’

‘‘All right,’’ Joe said. ‘‘But there is a number five.’’

Kate rolled her eyes. ‘‘Let me have it.’’

‘‘Mom will have a fit.’’

Kate decided to get that fit over with, and went to visit her mother and father the following afternoon. As it was a sunny, warm day, Kate’s parents were sitting in the yard after doing some gardening. Her father, Peter Mortimer, was slim and balding, wearing khaki shorts and a green golf shirt. Esther, who had short light brown hair, wore similar shorts and a blue shirt. They were both golf fanatics and were planning an early retirement.

Her mother hugged her hard. ‘‘Oh, Kate, how are you doing, honey?’’

Kate wanted to cry, but she didn’t. ‘‘I’m fine, Mom, really.’’

‘‘I hope so. Come and tell me all about Fitz’s place. I’ll go get some iced tea and cookies.’’

Her mother’s cure for everything was iced tea

and cookies. Kate sat down with her father, who smiled at her as if he had thought the same thing.

As her mother bustled out with the tray, she said, "Remember, Kate, don't tell my sister, Sadie, or brother Ron anything about this inheritance of yours. They'll be upset. As they are so much older, they remember all the goings-on. I was only a little child."

Kate nibbled on a cookie and explained Fitz's situation.

Her mother nudged Kate's father. "It's really a surprise, isn't it, Pete? Fitz being so rich and successful."

Peter Mortimer shrugged. "How can I say? I never met him. All I ever heard was that story about how he lost all your mother's grocery money at Belmont."

His wife gave him a look. "Well, he was a gambler. No doubt about it, I've heard." She looked once more at Kate. "I still don't see why he left the farm to you. I'm sure he had a child."

Kate was surprised by this information. "I haven't heard about a child."

"It's just something we all heard once. That's all."

Her father drained his tea. "You be careful, Katie. Horse racing can be a dirty business. I've read all those Dick Francis books."

Kate smiled. "Dad, that's fiction."

Her mother clucked her tongue. ‘‘Do as your father says, Kate, and be careful.’’ Esther frowned. ‘‘Are you really planning on racing horses, honey?’’

‘‘Yes.’’ Then she plunged in with the rest of her story about Rafe and the proposed business partnership.

‘‘A man you don’t even know,’’ her mother lamented. ‘‘Peter, talk to her.’’

‘‘I can’t say much if she’s made up her mind,’’ her father said.

‘‘Thank you, Dad. I’ve thought about it a lot and the more I think about it, the more I want to do it. Rafe hasn’t made up his mind yet, anyway. He might not agree to the partnership. But I definitely need a horse trainer and a manager, and he’s been doing it for Fitz for at least two years. He knew Nell before she died.’’

Her mother looked surprised. ‘‘He knew Nell, the wife?’’

‘‘Yes. He did. Just briefly. I’ve seen pictures of Uncle, Mom. He looked like a really nice man. I don’t think a nice man would hire a man like Rafe if he didn’t believe in him.’’

‘‘And where does he live. This Rafe?’’

‘‘Right now he lives on the property in a sweet little cottage. And he can stay there. It’s completely separate from the house. It’s convenient to the barn.’’

Peter shook his head. "Kate, don't do this because you think you owe a dead uncle something. Or because you've been, well . . . jilted."

"Well, I certainly don't intend to get married. I've made up my mind about that." Kate heard her mother sigh sorrowfully. "I can't go through this again, Mom. So why not give something to Uncle, Dad? It's shameful the way Mother's family behaved with him. He might have been a gambler once upon a time, but his gambling ways made a success of him. He found a woman he loved and lived a good life. After what has happened to me, that means something."

"I tend to agree with you," her father said, looking at his wife. "I always thought it was a pity she had a brother she never knew."

"I don't remember him much," Esther said. "It is sad that he's gone without us knowing him."

"Exactly," Kate said triumphantly. "So this is our chance to make amends to him."

Esther shook her head at her daughter. "I suppose I don't really mind. As long as we can come out to see the farm and this man before anything goes through."

"Promise, Mom," Kate said. But she was determined now. She owned a farm. Therefore, why not capitalize on her inheritance? As far as Rafe was concerned, if he decided to become her partner, then it would truly be a business deal only. Even if he was the best-looking man she had ever met.

Chapter Four

Kate's lawyer was a friend of her father's, a middle-aged man named Graeme Pollard. When she had contacted Rafe to tell him that her deal could go through, he was quite willing to negotiate a partnership in the business side of the farm. After Graeme had talked to him and gone out to the farm for a meeting, he phoned Kate.

"I thought the place was amazing, Kate," Graeme said. "I had a long meeting with Colson. He seems aboveboard. He has some extra cash to invest, enough to get you started. He mentioned something about a couple of big wins last year with your uncle. Although," Graeme chuckled. "He's not agreeable to you owning and him being the hired hand—his words."

"I know how he feels," Kate said wryly, wondering if she was really doing the right thing by including Rafe in her deal. And for the first time since her visit to the farm, she actually felt some doubt about her plans "So is he agreeable to a partnership?"

"Fifty-fifty. Nothing less. Is that what you want?"

She supposed if she was going to get out, it had to be now. But that would be cowardly, especially in light of the fact she had been so enthusiastic with her family and had sworn she could cope.

"Kate?" Graeme asked. "Are you there?"

"Yes. Graeme. Fifty-fifty. That's what I want."

"Okay. I'll draw up the papers. And then you can both come in and sign them. Let's see." Kate heard some rustling. "How about next Tuesday?"

"That's fine," Kate told him.

The Tuesday meeting meant that Kate needed to phone Rafe. She tried that evening but got no answer. Imagining him out in the barn tending to Talisman, she watched TV until about an hour had passed, then called again. He still wasn't there. What if he was out on a date? For a second her stomach sank. What if he did go out on dates quite a bit? What if he went out on dates when she was living at the farm? Could she stand to see him with another woman?

She jumped up from her chair, TV program forgotten.

What do you mean, another *woman, Kate? You're not* his *woman to begin with. So there is no* other. *This is a business deal, a partnership. You go your way and he goes his. That's how it will work.* Besides, she didn't want to get involved with another man. She was still mourning Casey.

Rafe was in the next time she phoned, but she didn't ask where he'd been. She stuck to business. "I've talked to my lawyer," she told him. "And if you want to meet me next Tuesday we can go and sign the papers."

"Great," he said, but she thought he sounded cool.

"You're okay with this?" she asked because suddenly *she* wasn't. It was a huge undertaking, going to live in a big farmhouse and run a horse farm. What had she been thinking?

"I'm fine with it, Kate. It's what I want."

Then why he didn't he sound on top of the world? His coolness chilled her own excitement. "Good," she told him, and they made arrangements for him to meet her in the parking lot of Graeme's office block on Tuesday afternoon.

She went into work the next morning intending to give her notice. Her assistant manager, slim, smart, dark-haired Lucy Brent, looked sad when Kate told her the plans.

"I'll miss you so much," Lucy said. "Imagine who we might get stuck with as a manager."

"What about you, Lucy? You know the job. You do it when I'm away."

"Do you think it would be offered?"

"I'll make a recommendation to Frank."

"Oh, would you, Kate? But I'll still miss you."

Kate wandered around the racks of stylish clothes in the store, stroking silk and crisp cotton fabrics that were new in for summer, and thought she would probably miss her job as well. While she did love clothes, it was mostly the challenge of making the store work that had been the best part of the job. As it was a privately owned store in a mall of corporate chain stores, she took pride in her work and the service they gave to customers. Their store motto was: "Our Clothes Last Forever," which was why Forever was the name of the store.

Frank Tilby, the elderly owner, was also sad to have her resignation.

"I think Lucy will be fine," he said, when she mentioned that her assistant would be a perfect replacement. "But you've been the person who has kept us going through difficult times. You've kept the store young in flavor."

"Thank you, Frank, but . . ."

"I know. We all have to move on."

And she did, Kate decided when she was back in the store. She did have to move on. There was no other way she could exist in this same life without being married to Casey.

On Tuesday Kate dressed in a blue suit with a slim short skirt and a jacket that nipped her waist. She left her hair loose and wore high heels. Her heart pounded as she drove over to Graeme's office. Whatever she told herself to the contrary, Rafe Colson was an attractive man whom a woman felt the need to impress.

She parked in the lot of the small office block and sat in the car to wait. She brushed her hair and put on some lipstick, wishing she had brought a book to read. She checked her appearance in the rearview mirror. She wasn't usually so fussy about how she looked, but today she wanted to make sure she had a mature business air about her, when inside her stomach roiled around with nervousness. She wasn't sure by now whether it was nervousness about the business deal or because she was seeing Rafe again. Oh surely she wasn't so shallow that she could be in love with one man, enough to marry him, and then be having butterflies about another man the moment the marriage was off? No, she wasn't that shallow. This was strictly business. She was having butterflies about the huge project she was about to undertake.

The black Jeep drove into the spot beside her while she wasn't paying attention. She looked over, and Rafe smiled at her through the window, his white teeth devastating. She smiled tightly back, and gathering her purse from the passenger seat, she slipped from her car and locked the door. Rafe was already beside her door. Wearing a dark suit, a white shirt and a blue tie, he looked so different, she stared at him.

''What's wrong?'' He touched his well-smoothed hair gingerly. ''Hair out of place?''

''No. It's just the suit I think.''

His smile showed an actual twinkle in his eyes. ''Didn't you think I owned one?''

''Not really.''

He gave her an appraising look. ''You look very nice as well. Very businesslike.''

Kate's heart sank. He knew her ploy. What was the use?

Hands in his pockets now, Rafe glanced around him. ''So shall we go in and get the business over with?''

Kate nodded. ''Yes. Graeme's office is on the second floor.''

They had to climb upstairs to reach the office. Kate went up first, Rafe following. She was so aware of him that her pulse hammered. She thought it might be his suit that was making her react to him. He looked so handsome, any woman would take second and third peeps at him.

When they reached Graeme's floor, she was telling herself, however much Rafe attracted her, she wasn't going to give into that attraction. She didn't want love again. Besides, he only wanted a horse lover, a woman who had probably been born with horse blood in her veins. She had visions of a lovely woman, wearing a Stetson, riding over a field on a beautiful, sleek horse. Not her. That was for sure.

"This way," she said and rushed along the corridor, past open doors, other offices and smiling receptionists. Graeme's door had a gold strip on it with his name on it, and she pushed it open.

Graeme's personal assistant's name was Cheryl Darlington, a nice woman in her thirties who had remained faithful to Graeme for the past ten years.

"Hi, Kate," Cheryl said and smiled warmly as Kate introduced Rafe. "Pleased to meet you, Rafe. Take seats. Graeme's just on the telephone with someone."

They sat down beside one another in the waiting area. Kate crossed her legs, and Rafe sat with his palms pressed over the sharp creases on his knees.

"It's only a partnership signing," she said.

He glanced at her. "Why would you say *only*?"

"Because I feel so tense about it."

An eyebrow rose. "Having second thoughts, cold feet?"

"No. But you were right from the start; it's a big undertaking."

"Which is exactly why we're going to share the responsibility, Kate."

"Of course."

He reached over and took hold of her hand. He lifted it off her lap, and he squeezed her fingers. "You do have cold hands, though."

Kate noticed Cheryl glance discreetly and then return her eyes to her computer screen. But she didn't care; she needed Rafe's support. Therefore, she kept her hand firmly in Rafe's warm one until Graeme came out of his office and ushered them inside.

Rafe's hand was on her waist as they went into the lawyer's office. He pulled out a chair for her. He was being so considerate. But then he was a considerate person. Hadn't he fixed her tire, fed her dinner and breakfast, and made sure she was safe for the night? She noticed that Graeme was watching them closely, and she smiled at her father's friend. *Business, Kate,* she reminded herself. *Otherwise Graeme will wonder what's going on, and he'll tell your father, and your parents will try to thwart the deal because they'll think something is brewing between you and Rafe, when nothing is happening at all.*

For an event she had spent a day or two preparing herself for, the deal didn't take long to conclude. Kate stuffed the papers into her spacious purse as they went downstairs again.

Rafe tucked his copy into his inside pocket. "I saw a restaurant a couple of blocks that way," he said. "Do you want to walk over and grab some coffee? A sort of celebration to seal the deal?"

She couldn't very well say no just because she found it difficult being in his presence. She was going to be with him day in and day out for the next while. She hadn't really understood what this partnership really meant, she decided. Or was it that she hadn't really noticed the first time they'd met how powerfully Rafe attracted her?

Along the sidewalk, her heels clicking, his soft-soled shoes a mere squish, she felt exposed with him. She was so aware of him, it was as if there were an electric pulse between them. She looked at him, but he walked easily, seemingly unaware of her.

"Do you want that, Kate?"

"Coffee?" She pumped her head up and down. "Yes. Love some."

The restaurant was cool from air-conditioning. They sat at a table near the window. Rafe ordered coffee and a muffin, and Kate ordered only coffee. A muffin would have stuck in her throat and choked her. She pushed her golden hair back over her shoulder.

Rafe lifted his coffee mug. "To the success of the farm."

She lifted her mug. "To success." Then she laughed. "Do you think Uncle Fitz would approve of this?"

"Absolutely," Rafe said. "I wouldn't be surprised if this was at the back of his mind."

"What? To get us together?" She realized what she had said; it sounded as if she meant they should be together as a couple.

As if to prove he wasn't reading anything into their relationship, Rafe took it generally. "Possibly. He wanted the house to stay in the family, so he left the farm to you and left me to deal with everything until you came to claim the inheritance."

"But he couldn't be certain we would go into a partnership."

Rafe shrugged. "No. He couldn't be certain. But it makes sense."

Kate nodded. "It does. He knew that you were determined to race Talisman and wouldn't like the idea of not being able to do that." She raised an eyebrow. "He probably knew you would try to persuade me to make the right decision."

“I never persuaded you.”

“Not directly. But I could tell you didn't really want to go.”

“My racing heart on my sleeve,” Rafe said wryly. “How's your heart?”

“My broken heart?” she asked.

He nodded. “Is it feeling better?”

“If I don't think about what happened.” Tears rushed into her eyes, and she brushed them away. “I can't help this. I shouldn't even talk about it. I try not to think about it. But I soak my pillow every night.”

“Poor little you,” he said softly. “The farm might do you good.”

“I want it to do me good. I want it to be a cure.”

He moved his mug around on the table like a chess piece. “Nothing is a cure but time. However, I found after Jennifer died that the land and the horses were a wonderful outlet.”

“But you didn't love her.”

“Not passionately,” he admitted. “But I cared a lot. I liked her. And she was beautiful, young, vibrant, with a big future in her chosen career.”

“Which was?”

“She was training to be a doctor.”

“Oh dear.” Kate reached across the table to touch his hand this time, the way he had touched hers back in the cottage when they shared his chili.

He turned her hand into his and let her fingers lay there. ''Did you have a ring?'' he asked.

''A small diamond.''

He rubbed the finger where the diamond used to be. ''Did you give it back to him?''

Her throat liquid with tears, she nodded. She had thrown it in typical jilted-lover style, and Casey had to crawl on his knees to find it.

''Tell me?''

Kate told him and he laughed.

''Serve him right, but diamonds are too cold, I think.'' Rafe met her gaze. ''A stone as blue as your eyes would be better for you.''

''Well. It will never happen,'' she said huskily. ''I'm not planning on falling in love ever again.''

They strolled back to the cars after their coffee. Beside his Jeep, Kate lifted her keys from her purse. ''Well, I'll see you again soon, Rafe.''

''Do you know how long exactly?''

''About a month. I've given my resignation at work. Luckily I had no lease on my apartment, so a month's notice is fine. I'll let you know how it goes. Possibly I'll be bringing my family out to the farm to have a look before I move in.''

''I'll make sure everything is ready for them.''

''Thank you. I would appreciate that.''

Rafe put out his hand. Kate enfolded her fingers into his. He had been cool since the restaurant. After she had told him she would never fall in love again, he had taken some money from his wallet to pay for their coffee, and he had stood up.

"Let's go," he had said.

Therefore, she expected him to briskly shake her hand, then turn around and open the Jeep door, but instead he drew her gently forward. With a slow-motion feeling, he lowered his mouth to hers and kissed her very thoroughly.

"Sealed the deal," Rafe said with a strange expression on his face. "See you, Kate."

He moved abruptly away from her, opened the Jeep and climbed in. She saw him loosen his tie and rake his fingers through his hair before he started the engine. She didn't wait around to watch him back out his vehicle or drive to the road. She went to her own car and got inside. *Deal sealed,* she thought. The weird expression on Rafe's face after he had kissed her had been enough to tell her that's all the kiss had been. It was all she wanted, anyway. Then why did she feel his very thorough kiss still on her mouth?

With her fingertips, she touched her lips and closed her eyes. In one breath she had stated very firmly that she would never fall in love again; in the next she was sitting here wondering why Rafe's kiss made her want more.

* * *

"I understand what you mean," her mother said when Kate took her family to see the farm about a week before she was due to move in. "Look at this house, Pete. It's huge."

"I *am* looking," Kate's father said as he stepped out of the car and looked up the vast stone walls. "Are you sure it's not too big for you, Kate?"

"Of course it is," she said wryly. "But there are people to help around the place."

Her mother frowned. "Are you sure you can afford all this?"

"Horse racing is a business. I'm starting my own business. And the house is mine, no mortgage."

Her father knocked on the stone wall. "Certainly solid. It's a great house, Kate. I have to agree. And of course, it *is* yours. No mortgage to worry about is a great help. I know because ours was paid off last year."

"Exactly," Kate said.

"I'm not worried about the house," Joe said. "I'm worried about the other half with that man."

"You'll meet him soon, and you'll see he's fine," Kate informed her brother.

"I'm with Joe. I do hope you know what you're doing," her mother said.

Alan Baker, the burly, middle-aged male half of the housekeeper duo, who had been at the gate to open it, beckoned them to the open door, and a lady with neat dark hair, wearing slacks and a blouse, came out to greet them.

"This is my wife, Shirley," he said. "This is Kate and her family, Shirl."

Kate walked up the steps and introduced her family, who were straggling behind her. "We've come to have a preview of the house and farm."

Shirley nodded. "We've been getting it ready for you. Come in and look around. Rafe's over in the barn, I think."

"I can't wait to meet Rafe," Kim whispered to Kate as they all went inside the house.

Joe gave her a glare, and Kate grinned. "He'll be competition for you, Joe, except he only goes for women who share his passionate interest in horses."

"That lets me out," Kim said, clutching her husband's arm. "But what about you, Katie? You're a horse person now."

"Not the way Rafe is, believe me." Kate grinned. "Besides. We're business partners. And that's the way it's going to stay." She raised her hand to her throat. "I've had it up to here with love." But she couldn't stop remembering Rafe's very thorough kiss the day of the paper signing. She found her mind becoming confused with kisses. Casey's kisses were the ones she should be remembering, not a man's she had only met a few weeks ago. A man who had kissed her once, to seal a business deal.

Accompanied by many oohs and aahs they toured the house. Then Kate led the way over the meadow. She noticed Alan was now on a tractor mower cutting the grass, and there were many more trucks around the property this time. Some horse trailers stood to one side. The fields were occupied by other horses, the rest of her thoroughbred stock, she thought. *Wow.*

"I thought you only had one horse, Katie?" her father asked.

"The house came with the stock."

"Oh my," her mother said. "This is a big operation. And my thinking, or being led to believe, that Fitz was just a small-time gambler, a loser. How wrong one can be about people."

Kate tucked her arm through her mother's. "I even think Aunt Sadie and Uncle Ron will be surprised. They're so materialistic, anyway, that this will appeal to them."

"Kate, you are bad to say that," her mother said. "But you're right."

Rafe wasn't in the barn, but Talisman was in his stall. None of her family were horse-oriented enough to bother with him too much. Kate patted him gently, the way Rafe had showed her that first day, and it made her remember his warm hand circling her wrist.

Poor little you, he had said in the restaurant and looked so sorry for her.

"The horse is pretty nice," Joe said, coming back to the stall. "The whole place is pretty nice."

"I'll say," her father agreed.

Kate heard a movement by the barn door and saw Rafe there. Her heart began to beat with the sound of his leather boot soles on the concrete as he walked toward them. She noticed Kim take in his long, blue-jean-covered legs and dark blue shirt, and her sister-in-law rolled her eyes at Kate. Kate stood stiffly, thinking, *Business Partner. That's what he is. What he has to be. It's only sensible. You're on the rebound, Kate. That's all these feelings are. You're confused.*

Kate introduced her family and was pleased that Rafe was charming to them.

"We've just come to see what she's getting into," Peter said.

"She's getting into a lot." Rafe's gaze rested on Kate's face. "Ready for the challenge?"

"Definitely," she said with a big grin. Did he remember that kiss the way she did?

"Kate's always ready for a challenge," Joe inserted. "She likes to take chances."

"Scared the dickens out of me when she was a little girl," her mother told Rafe.

"That's good. It's the type of personality you need for the horse racing business." Rafe smiled around the group. "I was thinking, we should all get to know one another. So I arranged a dinner tonight that Shirley is preparing. If that's all right?"

"That's thoughtful, Rafe," Esther said. "How nice. We are a little concerned about Kate, you'll understand."

"I understand. But everything will be fine. I'll do my best to make the business work for her."

Peter patted Rafe's arm. "That's good, son. Dinner sounds very agreeable."

Rafe glanced at Kate. "Okay with you?"

She nodded vigorously. "Oh, yes. Fine." She was really grateful to him for being so thoughtful about her family, almost as if he had guessed their reservations about her new enterprise.

"When are you moving in?" Rafe asked her as her family went ahead out of the barn.

"In a week."

"Everything will be in order here. Marc, my brother, is helping me, although he's not here today. His girlfriend, Crystal Summers, is a groom, so she's also helping out. I'm paying their salaries, as money's no problem. Fitz left a bank account to keep the farm running. It'll last well past your move-in date. Then our deal kicks in.'' He smiled at her. ''I'm just pleased I don't have to move.''

He seemed genuinely happy about the decisions they had made, and his smile sent everything inside her fluttering madly. Kate couldn't understand it. When she thought she was dead inside, Rafe could bring her emotions to life. She was really going to have to get a grip on those feelings. She needed to recover from Casey, from her loss. And when she was cured, she didn't want to be in love again. Ever. She had definitely made up her mind about that.

''Aren't you pleased?'' Rafe asked into her silence.

''Oh. Yes. I'm really excited. It's nice that your brother and his girlfriend can help.''

''I hoped you wouldn't mind my bringing them in, but I can't deal with all these horses myself.''

''I understand, Rafe. It's fine. Do what you see fit to deal with the horse side of the business.'' She didn't add *because I don't really know much about it yet*. She didn't want to cause hostility when there was none, and he was looking at her with a very intense stare that kept her heartbeat frantic.

They moved from the barn into the fresh air. Her family had strolled up to a fence where a number of other horses were grazing in the field.

"You better join them, Kate," Rafe said. "I'll see you at dinner."

The breeze blew her hair, and she brushed it aside with her hand. She could feel something palpable between them. "Dinner. Yes," she murmured. Then she turned quite blindly and ran across the field to join her family. Breathlessly, she clutched the top of the fence and looked at the horses until her fingers hurt from the pressure of holding on too tightly. *Get a grip. A big grip, Kate.*

Chapter Five

On moving day, a truck arrived at Kate's apartment first thing in the morning to take her possessions to her new home. The full extent of her excitement returned for her new venture when she was actually on her way. And she was so pleased that she now had her parents' blessing. Even though they still had reservations about the nature of the business, and her mother was wondering how she was going to tell Sadie and Ron the news, they had liked Rafe. At dinner, dressed in a crisp silver-gray shirt and slacks, he had been his most charming, a perfect business associate for their daughter.

Kate was about to press the buzzer when a man younger than Rafe loped down the driveway.

"Kate?" he asked as soon as he reached her.

She nodded.

"I'm Marc, Rafe's brother. I'll get the gate for you."

"Thanks, Marc," she called through the gate and watched him go into the gatehouse. He was shorter and more thinly muscular than Rafe, and probably in his very early twenties. But his hair was the same wavy texture. He wore jeans, T-shirt and a pair of scuffed black Western boots.

While she waited in the car, Kate figured she was going to have to do something about the gates. She disliked the idea of having to summon someone each time she left the house or came home.

When Marc had let her in, she parked in front of the house and climbed out of the car. It was a warm, sunny day and everything was green and lush. She opened the trunk to pull out some of her belongings. She was struggling with a box caught beneath the trunk rim when Marc joined her again. He easily extracted the box from the trunk.

"Do you want me to carry this stuff in for you?"

"If you don't mind. Although I can manage some of it."

Kate opened the front door of her new home, and they carried the boxes and suitcases into the foyer. "Thank you, Marc. Are you staying on here now?"

"Yes. It looks like it. Great to know the farm is going to keep running. Rafe's thrilled."

"He really is?"

"Yes, he really is. He hasn't stopped talking about you, but then I can see why. You're pretty cute."

Kate hid her confusion at the compliment behind a smile. "Thank you, but I'm not sure that's the reason he hasn't stopped talking about me. It's just business between us."

"Even so, he's hyped. Rafe is very conscientious. He's really been trying to prove himself as a horse trainer over these past few years, so this career boost is excellent news for him. I'm sure you guys will work it out. Fitz had a good reputation, so you can ride on his coattails." Marc moved to the door. "Anyhow. I'd better get out of here and not keep you. I'll let Rafe know you're here."

Kate's heart began to beat a little faster at the thought of seeing Rafe once more, and she kept herself busy by picking up a couple of bags of luggage to take upstairs. She wasn't sure what bedroom she wanted yet, so she left everything in the room she had slept in the first night. There was a honk outside, and she looked through the window to see the huge moving truck draw up into the driveway. She ran downstairs to open the front door. The driver, a stout man, came to the door holding a slip of paper for her to sign.

"I'm gonna need help," the driver said as Kate signed. "My assistant called in sick today with a virus. Is that your husband, the guy who opened the gate?" He pointed to Rafe in jeans, black T-shirt and sneakers, coming across the lawn. "I'll go get him to help me."

The man hurried off in Rafe's direction. Kate ran after him, waving the delivery slip. "Please, no," she said into the wind. "He's not my husband."

Not hearing her, the man reached Rafe and chatted to him for a moment. Rafe walked back with him to Kate. As the driver strolled leisurely to the truck, Kate put her hand on Rafe's arm. "You don't have to help him."

"It'll quicken things up if I do help," he said. "He doesn't look like the fastest guy in the world. Besides, he thinks I'm your husband."

Kate could feel color suffusing her face. "I tried to tell him."

To her surprise, Rafe grinned and leaned over, blowing a kiss onto her cheek. "Wife," he whispered, before he moved away to join the man at the rear of the truck.

With Rafe helping and Kate directing, it didn't take long for the moving van to empty. Kate signed the bill and the big truck roared away.

Rafe went to close the gates, and Kate stood on the step watching him. He really was a lot of help.

When he returned, he said. "Come on. I'll help you get organized. *Wife.*"

"You won't let that go, will you?" Kate said, surprised to find herself sound so irritable. If everything had gone as planned, she *would* have been a wife.

Rafe touched his forehead. "Sorry, Kate. I forgot."

She brushed her hair back from her face. "It's okay. You can mention words like wife, marriage, love . . ." her voice faltered. "Around me."

He ushered her indoors. "I won't do it again. I'll fix the coffee to make up for it."

Rafe made himself quite at home in her new kitchen, using her coffeemaker and a package of fresh coffee she'd brought along.

"You're so domestic," she said, opening a tin of homemade cookies her mother had sent with her. She set the tin on the table.

"I've had to be. I left home when I was sixteen and lived on the backside of tracks for years. I took my college degree by correspondence. Then I settled on a farm in Kentucky, where I helped the trainer."

She remembered he had told her he was from

Ellis Corners. ‘‘When did you come back to New York then?’’

‘‘My Dad had a heart attack a few years ago, so I came home to be closer to the family and luckily got this job with Fitz.’’

‘‘Is your father okay now?’’

‘‘He’s fine. He stopped smoking and lost weight. But he doesn’t work anymore. He used to run the hardware store. He sold out when he got ill. Mom works there now. Marc has an apartment over their garage, so he keeps an eye on them. You’ll meet them. They drive out here for the day sometimes.’’

‘‘I’ll look forward to meeting them,’’ Kate told him, meaning it. It would be interesting to meet Rafe’s parents. In some ways it would help to identify him for her. Right now he was still very much her uncle’s employee, even though they were legally business partners.

‘‘Do you have some coffee mugs?’’ Rafe asked.

Kate found two mugs in a box, unwrapped them, and rinsed them at the sink. She dried them with some paper toweling, thinking that each time they met they became a little friendlier, and she found it easier to be with him.

Rafe poured the coffee into the mugs, then chose a cookie from the tin. ‘‘Did you make these?’’

"No, my mother did."

"Your mother's a nice lady, Kate. Fitz would have liked her. It's a pity that family differences keep people apart."

"It is," Kate agreed, feeling sad. "But we can't do much about it. They were from a different generation. But now Fitz is back in the family."

Rafe picked up another cookie. "I'm beginning to believe that was Fitz's wish. He took a gamble with us, the artful old man."

Kate met his gaze and smiled at him. "Well, he was a gambling man. Why not also gamble with his will? I think you might be right."

After the coffee, Rafe helped Kate arrange her few pieces of furniture between her uncle's antique collection. He stacked all her boxes into one area of the dining room, so she could unpack when she had time.

When they were finished she said, "I really appreciate your help, Rafe."

"It would have taken you a long time alone, and some of those boxes were heavy."

"They're full of books," she said. "I keep every book I've ever had since I was a kid."

"Have you read them all?"

"Some fifty times," she admitted, making a sheepish face.

"I've got a few of those as well," he also admitted. ‘‘Do you want to come over for dinner? Marc and Crystal have set up the barbecue, and I think we’re having steamed fish.’’

‘‘That sounds very healthy.’’

‘‘Crystal’s into feeding Marc healthy foods because of the heart-attack factor in the Colson men. Do you like fish?’’

‘‘I love fish.’’ Kate didn’t feel like eating by herself from a can. ‘‘All right. Do I have to change?’’

‘‘No way. We certainly don’t stand on formality here.’’

Rafe grinned at her as they walked across the meadow to the cottage. Kate smiled back, deciding that maybe this partnership was going to be fine.

They went into the cottage, and from the little courtyard came the aroma of a barbecue. Crystal greeted them. She was a pretty redhead, wearing jeans and a shirt.

Rafe introduced Kate.

‘‘Pleased to meet you.’’ Crystal shook her hand. ‘‘And thank you for keeping the farm and giving us employment.’’

Kate really hadn’t thought of that aspect of her inheritance. ‘‘Did you work here before?’’

‘‘All the time. Loved your uncle, Kate. He was a real sweetie.’’

Rafe disappeared to wash up for the meal, and

Crystal led Kate through to the courtyard where Marc was barbecuing.

"My specialty, Kate," Marc said, waving a long-handled spatula around.

Crystal rolled her eyes. "Sure it is. I prepared the fish; all you're doing is standing over it. Don't we sound like an old married couple already?"

Kate nodded, wondering if she would ever have gotten to that stage with Casey. They had never sounded like an old married couple. Not even an engaged couple, when she thought about it.

"Are you engaged?" she asked Crystal.

"No, but we've been going out for a lifetime. We went to high school together."

"Are you going to get married?"

"Oh, probably, eventually."

"That's great," Kate told her, although she felt a little sadness in her heart. She really had wanted to get married. Maybe she had wanted it too much and chosen the wrong man.

Rafe joined them, and they sat around on chairs, eating and chatting. Crystal, who had grown up with horses, was as knowledgeable about the animals and the racing scene as the two brothers. Kate tried to take in all they were saying about horses and the farm, but it didn't make too much sense. But it would make sense eventually, she decided. She was going to make sure it made sense. She was here now. She had a library full of books to read. And a farm to run. She was ready to learn.

The clanking and scraping noises Kate recalled from her very first early morning at the farm woke her up. For a while she snuggled beneath the comforter, then remembering she had boxes to unpack, she reluctantly got up, showered and dressed, tied her hair into a ponytail and set to work. When the contents of the boxes were stored and the dust sheets had been removed from all the furniture and neatly packed away, Kate strolled from room to room, admiring all her new belongings.

In the dining-room sideboard she found the silver cutlery, crystal, beautiful china and Fitzhenry Farm monogrammed tablecloths and napkins that Shirley had impressed her family with when they all ate dinner at the long oak table. She should really throw a housewarming party. Her family would love to visit the farm again, and she had some friends who wanted to see the farm as well. She could also invite Aunt Sadie and Uncle Ron. It might be a chance for them to see what a success Fitz had been. Deciding the housewarming was a good idea, Kate planned to buy invitations when she went to the market later.

After a sandwich lunch, Kate drove to the

gates, forgetting that she didn't know how to open them. She didn't want to bother Rafe. She needed to show him that she could do everything herself, and that their venture was going to run smoothly. Climbing out of the car, Kate went inside the gatehouse. There was a large wheel to work the gates. It took all of her strength, but she managed to open one gate, enough space for her to drive through.

Feeling that she had jumped one hurdle, Kate drove to Ellis Corners. It was a small town that was close to a lake and a downhill ski resort, so there were many antique and craft stores. The supermarket was large and well stocked. All the time Kate shopped, Rafe was in her mind. She hadn't seen him yet today, but at least she knew she could leave the farm in his capable hands. When she walked past the hardware store, she thought about him again and wondered if his mother was working there today. She also wondered where his parents lived in town. There were some lovely properties along the lakeshore.

Kate found the gate was tightly closed when she returned. She really had to do something quick about this gate problem. She pressed her finger to the buzzer, wondering who actually heard it. After her first visit, when Rafe had responded, Alan and Marc had both been waiting for her arrival the other times. Alan wasn't here today, and she hadn't seen Marc either. Then she saw Rafe striding toward her. He looked annoyed with her.

"Did you close the gate?" she called to him when he was close enough.

"Yes. I did. Kate, never leave the gate open. Why didn't you call me to open it properly, and then close it behind you?"

"I didn't think." She couldn't understand why he was in such a state about the gate.

When the gate opened, she drove through and up to the front door. She opened the trunk and took out her parcels.

Rafe joined her. "Just make sure you have someone open and close the gates when you leave," he said.

Kate settled the packages in her arms. "Why?"

"For security reasons. We have some expensive horses on the premises."

She hadn't thought of that. "I'm sorry. I didn't think. But we'll have to come up with a different deal for the gates. I can't be buzzing all the time."

"Maybe we should have a more modern opening method. Let's look into it. Maybe you can."

"All right. I will."

"I'll see you later then," Rafe said.

"Probably. Thanks." She made a face at his

back as he strode around the side of the house. Sometimes Rafe was far too serious.

Kate spent the rest of the day working on the house. After a light dinner, she took her invitations into Uncle Fitz's office. Sitting behind the vast oak desk, she felt thrilled that all her business would take place in this pleasant paneled and leather room. When she had a moment, she would set up her computer and get the business underway. Although she did realize she really didn't have a clue as to how to operate a horse farm.

She wrote all the invitations and drew a map to enclose with them. On the bottom of each invitation she added her new phone number. When the envelopes were ready, she slipped a rubber band around them, ready to mail the next day. Then she phoned her parents and talked to her mother, telling her about the upcoming party.

"I'm not sure Ron and Sadie will attend," Esther said. "But it's worth a try. I would really like it if the family became settled on the issue of Fitz."

"Have you talked to them?"

"No. Just send them the invitation. Maybe a little note about what happened to clarify things, Kate."

Kate agreed with her mother and did just that.

Kate wrote down a few ideas for the buffet menu, and as she was writing, she heard a knock on a door. Carrying her pen, she left the office, listened and heard the knock again. It was the kitchen door. She walked through the kitchen, down the narrow dark hallway that she felt needed another light, and opened the door to Rafe.

"Hi," she said. "Are there any problems?"

He put his hand on the doorpost in a rather aggressive stance. "Where have you been this afternoon?"

Kate heard an accusation in his tone but said lightly, "Fixing up the house."

His expression was impatient. "I thought you were my business partner."

"I am, Rafe. What's the matter?"

"We have things to discuss."

Kate glanced at her watch. "Well, it's a bit late. Would tomorrow be all right?"

For a second he appeared as if he were going to dispute her, but then he let go of the doorpost and stepped back into the darkness. "I guess it will have to be all right. See you tomorrow."

Kate frowned as she fastened the back door. His irritation had been more stifled than when he had opened the gate, but he had definitely been annoyed with her. Why? He couldn't possibly be annoyed about Talisman anymore because she had righted that. His dream for racing Talisman, and all the other horses, was back in place. And, in many ways, he had an even better deal than he had with her uncle. He had a partnership in the farm.

Feeling completely confused by the man, Kate returned to Fitz's office and closed down for the night. But Rafe plagued her dreams, so she got up early and ate her breakfast sitting in the room overlooking the swimming pool. She wondered if it might help relations to invite Rafe to the party.

Deciding anything to smooth out her life was worth a try, Kate walked outside into the sunny morning. She saw Marc and Rafe at the track, Rafe astride a white horse, Marc on Talisman. She walked across the meadow, enjoying the feel of the soft country air on her skin. She reached the fence where Rafe and his horse were. Kate thought he looked magnificent mounted above her.

Kate climbed up the fence to meet Rafe's height. She sat down on the railing and reached out to pat his white horse. "What's his name?"

Rafe looked at her. "Aspen."

Wearing a helmet, Marc cantered Talisman around the track past them.

"He's fast," Kate remarked.

"I hope so. This is Talisman's workout."

"Oh," she said, knowing she sounded obtuse. She shifted on the fence. "I just wanted to talk to you about a housewarming party I'm having. Friends, family, that type of thing."

His eyes narrowed. "I don't have much time for parties."

"Why ever not?"

Rafe's gaze was on Marc, who was moving Talisman into a full gallop now. Hooves thundered past them.

"We're running a business, Kate. This isn't a social exercise."

"I also live here now, Rafe. People I know want to see the farm. One party gets all those requests over at once."

"All right. But let's discuss it later," he said. "I'm working right now."

Kate tossed her head, her hair flying in the breeze, and vaulted from the fence. She ran back to the house. What was wrong with him? He had been fine when she first arrived. Now he was acting moody.

Kate wondered at her sense in making him her business partner. If he acted like this all the time, her life on the farm was going to be completely miserable. And hadn't she taken on this enterprise because it had come at just the opportune moment to get over her misery?

Wishing Casey had never left her, so he might be here with her, helping her, Kate went into the kitchen, picked up a glass she'd used earlier, slipped some ice into it and poured in a canned soft drink. She was taking her first sip when Rafe walked in. He looked big and handsome in his jeans and riding boots.

"Don't knock or anything," she said grumpily.

Rafe shook his head. "I'm sorry, Kate. I shouldn't have gone off at you like that. Marc reminded me that you have to settle in."

She grimaced. "Marc's more thoughtful than you, that's why."

He inclined his head. "Probably that's the truth. It's just that this is a working farm. We have a race to prepare Talisman for, as well as some of the other horses. I feel we've wasted enough time. Talisman should have been running before now. There isn't time for parties."

"Well, I'm going to make time." She put her glass down on the counter and wiped her damp hands down the sides of her jeans. "It's only for one evening, and besides, I don't think we should interfere in one another's social life."

"I wasn't thinking I was interfering. But I guess I was." He rubbed the back of his neck. "I was out of order, Kate."

"You were," she said, meeting his eyes. She had the feeling there was something more to his mood than his explanation warranted. And for a second she thought he was going to move forward to touch her, but he didn't. He left her alone, feeling as if all her breath had been sucked out of her.

She finished off her drink and let out a long sigh. All aspects of Rafe puzzled her, as well as her own reaction to him.

That afternoon Kate went out to mail her invitations. She got Marc to open the gate, and she walked to the mail box she had seen at the end of the road. She didn't care if Rafe disapproved of her having a party. She was going to have it anyway. Still, she felt she should involve herself in the racing business as quickly as possible. Upon her return to the farm, Marc let her in again, and she went across the meadow. With the horses grazing in the fields and the bustle around the stables, Kate was sure Fitz would be pleased. As she couldn't see Talisman out in the paddock, she walked into the barn. Talisman was in his stall. Beside the stall were some treats, so she handed him a couple, and he ate them from her palm.

''Nice boy,'' she murmured.

''Good,'' Rafe said behind her. ''He let you near him.''

Kate twisted around. ''I'm lucky he didn't bite my hand off then. Just like you wanted to do earlier.''

Rafe made a face. ''I guess I asked for that.'' Then he laughed. ''Give me your hand then.''

She put out her hand. Rafe's lips touched her fingers with a row of butterfly kisses. "There. How's that?"

Kate swallowed hard. His touch vibrated through her. "That's fine."

"Good." Rafe let her fingers go, and he patted Talisman and cleared his throat. "Talisman wouldn't bite you either. He's not a biter. Springtime, down in the other stall, is a biter. So don't walk too close to her stall."

Kate stared into Talisman's eyes. "I won't."

There was a long silence, then Kate said, "I came here to deal with business?"

"Sure. Come this way."

Rafe led Kate into a comfortable office at the end of the barn near the tack room. It was eclectically furnished, as if every leftover piece of furniture from house and cottage had been put in there. The desk held a phone with an answering machine and a personal computer. Paperwork was neatly piled to one side. There were a coffeemaker and mugs on the window ledge.

Waving a hand around, Rafe said, "This is where I run the show."

"I didn't know this was here."

"Because you haven't been farther than the house since you moved in."

"Stop it, Rafe. Give me a chance, will you? I want to learn, but I have to settle."

He shook his head, more at himself than at her. ''Okay. Sit down in that chair near the computer and I'll show you what goes on.''

He might be temperamental, but as Rafe passed on his knowledge of the racing world, Kate knew she had gone into partnership with exactly the right person. He did leave her with a warning that horses didn't always meet their potential.

''You mean Talisman might not work out?'' she asked.

''Possibly that could happen. Usually there's another horse waiting in the wings. Not always with Talisman's potential, but sometimes horses you least expect to be great, are great. For instance, I had two big wins with Springtime last year.''

''The biter?''

''The biter.'' He clicked the computer mouse. ''These are all the races I've scheduled for this year. Talisman's are marked with the stars.''

Kate pointed to the screen. ''There's one coming up soon.''

''Yes. That's why I don't want to fool around with time. Horses only have a few good years. You can't shelve them and put them on hold.''

He knew she was referring to her party, but she didn't comment.

''Horses can also have injuries.'' Rafe placed his hand on the desk, his fingers moving like a horse's legs. "Imagine all that weight on such delicate legs."

She understood and wondered for a moment why she had entered into a business that could be so unpredictable, so fragile. Just like life. Hadn't her relationship with Casey been just as unpredictable, just as a fragile?

"We'll have big vet bills," Rafe said wryly.

"We'll deal with it, Rafe. We can't back out now, can we?"

He shook his head. "No. We can't. We're in it together." He turned his chair until he was facing her. "How's it going now?"

She knew what he meant. "I'm not crying so much. Coming here is taking my mind off everything. There aren't the memories."

"That helps a great deal." He touched her hair and ran his knuckle down the golden strands. "I want this to work out, Kate."

She trembled a little at his delicate touch. "It will. Promise. This is more real than love, Rafe. We have a house, a farm, the horses. It's much more real. I like that."

"Love can also be real," he said softly, still stroking her hair. "If both people want it badly enough and work at it. My parents, for instance. And yours, Kate. And Fitz and Nell. Loads of couples."

"I know. They're good examples, but I don't

think I'm up to it. I really don't. For some reason I had something inside me that made Casey panic."

"Or maybe he had something inside himself?"

"Possibly. His parents were divorced. He mentioned that a lot and I know it hurt him, even if he pretended he didn't care."

"Maybe that was it, Kate. Maybe he was frightened that divorce and all the bitterness would happen to him."

"Why didn't he say so then?"

"He might not have really known how his parents' divorce had affected him. I have a friend who has been engaged to the same woman for three years and won't commit because his mother and father split up. He's never come to terms with it. He thinks he's the same makeup."

"But Casey wasn't like that. He was very sure of himself. He also had someone else—I think that's what happened—he met a woman he loved more."

"Then he didn't love you enough, so you're best rid of him."

Kate tried to smile. "Sure I am, Rafe."

Rafe removed his hand from her silky hair with a gesture of reluctance. "Give it time."

She was, she thought as she strolled back across the meadow. She was giving her broken heart lots of time. Then why did she keep thinking about Rafe?

Chapter Six

The following morning Kate was up early, so she actually reached the barn before Rafe did. She had a good look around at all the horses. They appeared pretty smart and lively. But Talisman, she had to admit, possessed an extra presence. He gave her a look, with an added toss of his head, as if he knew he was king of charm.

"We are eager," Rafe said, walking toward her, long-legged and vitally male.

Kate's heart hammered in her ears. Was it possible to love two men? Could she fall in love with someone new while still nursing a broken heart? Or hadn't she loved Casey as much as she thought she had?

"I woke up early," she said, striving to keep her voice even and unemotional.

Marc said, joining them, "Don't listen to him, Kate. He's a workaholic."

"Who slept in this morning," Rafe said wryly as he went to let Talisman from his stall.

Kate joined the men at the track for Talisman's workout. Today she sat quietly, making no mention of parties. This was work. And she really enjoyed watching Marc ride Talisman. He was an expert rider and could control the horse in ways that Kate found awe-inspiring.

When Talisman was being hot-walked by Crystal outside the barn, Kate helped Rafe and Marc. There was so much to do with cleaning the stalls and working with the horses that she wondered how the farm would manage with only the four of them to handle everything. As she hung a hay ball close to Springtime's stall, the magnitude of the undertaking overwhelmed her once again. She quite understood Rafe's irritation when she seemed as if she were shirking her responsibility by planning a party instead of helping out. But she hadn't intended to seem that shallow. She just wasn't aware of what they had to do each day. So much of it was physical that she flopped into bed that night and slept right through for the first time since Casey had dumped her.

The following morning she was there to watch Talisman's workout and help around the barn once more. Crystal began to demonstrate ways to handle horses, and Kate thought she might eventually lose her fear of the big animals. She went back to the house for lunch around noon. She was slipping the dishes into the dishwasher when Louise Maxwell, a neighbor, phoned to invite her over for iced tea. Kate got Alan to open the gate and drove over. Louise, a slender, ash-blonde woman in her early thirties, who wore exquisite cream slacks and shirt, was waiting in the driveway outside her massive one-level home, merely a speck on the magnificent acreage of Maxwell Stables.

"I'm pleased to meet you, Kate. Come on through the house. We'll sit by the pool."

The pool was in a courtyard of the house, surrounded by fountains. While they made themselves comfortable in loungers by the sparkling water, Louise's maid served them drinks.

When the maid had left, Louise asked, "Rafe is working for you, I hear?"

To Kate it seemed as if Louise's question was the reason she had been invited over in the first place. Kate nodded. "Well, he's not exactly working for me. We've formed a partnership of the business side of the farm."

Louise's eyes widened. "Is that so? Did you know him before?"

"No. But he was working for my uncle, and

he has more expertise in horses than I do. It seemed to be the most practical way to do it.''

''I think you're being very astute. Rafe has a great future. And the Fitzhenry name is a legend in racing in these parts.''

Kate ran her finger down the side of the moist glass. Louise sounded so positive, and although Kate had been watching the way Talisman ran, she couldn't see herself taking her uncle's place in the racing world. ''I hope so.''

''Rafe will be one of the names to be reckoned with one day,'' Louise said. ''My husband, Bob, he thinks he's a good horseman.''

Kate smiled. ''That's great news.''

When their drinks were finished, Louise drove Kate in an open Jeep to the stables. There were many wonderful sleek horses, plus a staff working diligently. In the tack room was a litter of new kittens, and Kate knelt down to pet the bundles of fur.

''You can have a couple,'' Louise offered. ''We have too many cats around here already.''

''I like the black one and the white one.''

''Let me take a look.'' Louise picked each kitten up and inspected them. ''One male, one female. Perfect. Wait till the weekend, and then I'll get one of the grooms to bring them over.''

Kate reluctantly let the kittens go and got to her feet. ''Thank you. They're so cute.''

"I don't know what happened to Fitz's old cats. Likely they died."

"Did you know my uncle well?"

"We moved here from another farm, so we were only neighbors for a few years, but he did come here for a party or two. That's why I invited you over. I thought it would be nice to cultivate a friendship. We should be neighborly."

"That's very sweet of you. I agree," Kate told her and went home looking forward to the arrival of her kittens.

Kate planned to name the white female one Puff and the black male, Spark. She bought all the equipment and food she would need for the cats on her next trip to the market. On Saturday, after they were safely in her house, she impulsively went to find Rafe. He was in his office, using the computer.

She stood by the door for a moment, watching him work, wishing she hadn't been so impulsive. Why should Rafe care if she had kittens or not?

"Hi. Can I help you?"

"I was just around and I thought you might like to see the kittens Louise Maxwell let me have. Do you want to come and see them?" She sounded like a shy little girl asking the boy she had a crush on for a date.

"I didn't know you knew Louise."

"She invited me over for iced tea the other day, so we could get to know one another."

Rafe stood up. "That's nice of her. I met her a few times at the track."

Kate gave him an askew glance. "I wondered where she had met you. She said Fitz went to her parties."

"Yeah. Fitz went. I'd love to see the kittens, Kate. I'll walk over with you."

Relieved that he didn't think she was out of order, she smiled at him. "Thanks. I thought for a moment I shouldn't really have bothered you."

"It's okay, Kate. I like all animals."

But not parties, she thought as they left the barn. He had met Louise at the track, not at one of her parties. He had made that clear.

The kittens were rolled into little balls of sleeping fur in their basket. Rafe picked them up, and they looked so tiny in his hands. But he treated the little animals, as they became more playful and tried to climb his shoulder, with the same patience and gentleness as he did his horses.

Rafe deposited the bundles of fur on their cushion once more. "They're really sweet, Kate. Would you like a dog as well? I know someone who breeds golden retrievers."

"I'd love one, Rafe. A dog would be good to have around the farm."

They both stood up, Rafe reaching down automatically to help Kate to her feet. "We could go now to look at the puppies. You could choose one. Marc's here to look after things."

His touch stayed on her hand as he let it go. "If it's not taking you away from your work." Kate tried not to sound sarcastic.

"Most of my work is morning work. I can afford to take some time off."

Hardly believing that Rafe actually planned to relax for a while, Kate nodded. "All right. Fine. I'll just go grab my purse."

"And I'll bring the Jeep around the front."

Ten minutes later, Kate closed the front door and tucked herself in beside Rafe in his Jeep. While the interior of the vehicle wasn't exactly messy, there was no mistaking what Rafe did for a living. In the back was a heap of tack. Stuffed down the side pocket beside her were racing papers and programs. Everywhere on the upholstery and floor were strands of hay.

Kate chuckled. "Do you live in your Jeep with your horse?"

"I admit it needs to be cleaned out." Rafe eased back in his seat as he drove up the road away from the farm. "This is good—we have a moment—I wanted to talk to you to suggest we hire back more of Fitz's staff."

So this wasn't completely relaxation for him; his mind was always thinking *farm.* However,

Kate agreed with him. She recalled all the staff she'd seen running the Maxwell Stables, and the way she had thought the four of them wouldn't be able to cope for long alone. They would definitely need more help. "That sounds like a good idea, Rafe."

He stopped the Jeep at an intersection. "I'm pleased you think so. We have to agree on everything, Kate, this being a fifty-fifty business split."

"I understand. I thought the other day, what if someone in our small crew gets sick and can't be here?"

"Exactly. I'll work out who I think we need to hire, and then we can discuss it."

"That's fine," Kate said.

Rafe turned the Jeep into a farm gate, and they bumped up a driveway to a big two-floor farmhouse. The door opened on the porch, and a woman ran down the steps, wearing jeans and a T-shirt, long brown hair flying behind her.

"Rafe," she called out, and as soon as Rafe was out of the Jeep, he grasped her into his arms and hugged her.

Rafe tucked the woman under his arm. "Samantha, this is Kate, Arden's niece. My pardner."

Samantha smiled warmly and took hold of Kate's hands. "It's wonderful to meet you, Kate. Rafe has cheered up a hundred percent since you came along with this business enterprise. I'm so pleased.''

''Sam is my cousin,'' Rafe explained with a smile, and Kate was under the impression he had enjoyed teasing her with his pretty relative.

Sam moved closer to Kate. ''Rafe gave me a call to say you were coming here. I'll show you the puppies, Kate. They're just adorable.''

They *were* adorable. Kate chose her puppy from the litter, and they went into the house for some refreshment. It was a large, untidy house. Sam explained that her mother and father and two brothers also lived here. It was primarily a dairy farm, but they grew vegetables for market and ran strawberry-picking groups in the summer.

The puppy was rambunctious on the way home in the Jeep. Rafe and Kate were both laughing and licked to pieces by the time he parked outside the cottage. The dog leapt out and ran around in circles in the meadow.

''He's crazy,'' Kate wailed.

Rafe stood beside her. ''He's got plenty of room to run out here. His energy will sap eventually.'' Rafe swooped up the playful puppy. ''Come on. Be good to your new mistress.'' The puppy licked Rafe's jaw. ''What are you going to call him, Kate?''

''Fitz,'' she said. ''Because he looks like he's having fits, and he's unpredictable.''

"Fitz it is." Rafe handed the puppy to Kate. "Take him indoors and introduce him to the kittens."

Kate clutched Fitz in her arms. "I hope they love one another."

"I'm sure they will." For a moment Rafe gazed at Kate and Fitz, and then he glanced away. "Anyway, it's back to work. I'll make up a list of the staff we need, Kate."

Feeling as if his gaze had been torn away from her, she said breathlessly, "All right."

Rafe walked to the barn. Marc and Crystal met him by the door, and the three of them began to chat together. They knew one another from a long time ago, and Kate felt left out. Nevertheless, Fitz was urging her to get going, so she had no time to dwell on her loneliness. She took him into the house and let him loose on the kittens.

Alan Baker was in the kitchen, washing his hands.

"Who have you got here?" Alan asked.

"His name is Fitz."

"After your uncle?"

"Yes. Do you think that's appropriate?"

"Absolutely, Kate. He'd be tickled. The same way as he would be tickled to see his farm still going strong. It's a good thing you did, Kate. You kept a lot of us employed."

She realized that now. "I'm enjoying myself. It's such a new adventure. A different life."

She was certainly telling the truth. With the animals in the home, she felt as if she were in the midst of continuous scurrying paws. That night they all climbed the stairs and jumped onto her bed to sleep. It felt comforting to have them there.

With the party not far off, Kate began to plan the event. Shirley agreed to stay on to help but didn't accept Kate's invitation to join in.

"It's your thing," Shirley told her. "We're staff, after all. Besides, we'll be around anyway."

"But you can stay over in one of the bedrooms," Kate told her. "Then you don't have to worry about being late."

"We'll do that then," Shirley agreed.

As her party plans materialized, Kate realized she was a lone woman, a hostess without an escort. The guests consisted of her parents, Joe and Kim, Kate's friend Iris and her boyfriend, David, and Uncle Ron and Aunt Sadie and their spouses.

Great, Kate thought. If Rafe was coming he would be her partner. But he wasn't coming. And she should have invited Marc and Crystal. It wouldn't be fair if they saw a party going on without them.

She walked down to the barn and was pleased to see Crystal in one of the stalls. Crystal had her hair tucked into a baseball cap, and with her old T-shirt, jeans and rubber boots, she looked perfect for the job.

Kate mentioned the party.

"I would love to come," Crystal said. "And I'm sure Marc will as well. Thank you, Kate. Is Rafe coming?"

Kate shrugged. "He doesn't like parties."

Both of Crystal's eyebrows rose. "Since when?"

"Since forever, I presumed."

"That's not true. Of course he likes parties. He's messing with you, Kate. Go make him come. Tell him we'll be there."

"Do you know where he is?"

"In the tack room. Go on. Ask him."

Kate went to the tack room door. She hated to mention the party again.

Rafe saw her. "Hi, Kate. How's it going?"

"Fine." She stuck her fingers into her back pockets, thinking that if she had the guts to ask him to be her business partner when she barely knew him, she could invite him to a party. "I've just asked Crystal and Marc to the party, and they want to come. And as I haven't heard for sure from you, I thought I would ask once again. Just to make sure. Besides that, Rafe, it would be nice to introduce my business partner to my friends."

He hung a bridle on a hook. "In that case, I'll come."

"You mean if I treat it as if we're business partners, you'll come, but if I think it's something more personal, you won't?" Immediately after the question was asked, she knew she shouldn't have asked it.

He expelled a breath. "No. I'll come anyway, but you mentioned the business aspect."

"Of course. Because that's what we've got, isn't it? Unless you want to bring someone, of course." That would defeat the purpose. She would still be the odd one out.

He gave her a crooked look. "Are you bringing someone?"

"No. I'll be alone. Won't I?"

He smiled at her. "Am I to replace whatever-his-name-was?"

"No." Kate pressed her fingers to her forehead. "I'm just inviting you to a party, Rafe, and you're making a real big thing of it."

"No, I'm not, Kate. You're making a big thing of it. And I don't have anyone right now to bring, so I'll come alone as well. We'll make up the odd couple. Is that what you're thinking?"

She kicked her toe into the floor.

He grinned.

She shrugged. "It would save my pride."

"Exactly."

"But you don't have to be with me."

He raised an eyebrow. "But I *will* be with you." He walked over to her and placed his hand on her shoulder. He made her look into his eyes. "Kate. I want to come to the party. All right?"

She wanted to cry, for some reason, like she always wanted to cry when he was being sweet to her. *Poor little you.*

He impulsively kissed her nose. "Let me know if you need any help with the party."

"Okay. Thanks." They were the only words she could get out before she left his office. She stood in the barn for a while and breathed deeply. She was sure she was falling in love with him, but she didn't want to.

She gazed at Talisman. "What do you think?"

Talisman gave her a knowing stare.

She couldn't fall in love with Rafe. She just couldn't. She left the barn and found Crystal outside holding a pail beneath the outside faucet.

"What did he say?" Crystal asked above the sound of running water.

"He'll come."

Crystal turned off the tap. "There, I told you he would."

"Yes, you did."

"Do you like him?" Crystal asked.

"Of course I like him." And that was the absolute truth.

"No. I mean, do you dig him?"

Kate screwed up her nose. "Like a boyfriend?"

Crystal laughed. "Yes, like a boyfriend. Rafe doesn't date very much. He should be married at his age. It would be perfect if you two got married."

"Hold it, Crystal. We're business partners. We barely know one another." Why did those words sound so hollow?

"Get to know one another," Crystal said with a mischievous smile. "Begin at the party."

Chapter Seven

Kate shopped for two days and cooked for two more. On the day of the party, when she finally had the prepared food in the refrigerator, ready to be set out on the dining-room table, buffet style, she felt quite exhausted.

Shirley shooed her from the kitchen. ‘‘Go and get ready, Kate, and make yourself pretty.’’

Kate pushed back her tumbled hair and made a comical face. ‘‘You mean I don't look pretty now?’’

‘‘I didn't mean that. I meant make yourself look glamorous and give Rafe something to drool over.’’

Kate said what she repeated to herself like a mantra these days, ‘‘Rafe's my business partner, Shirley.’’

"Alan is my business partner, but we're married."

"Yes. But. Rafe wants a woman who's completely knowledgeable and shares his intense interest in horses." This was another thought that constantly went through Kate's mind, and why she certainly didn't want to fall in love with him.

Shirley wiped her hands on a towel. "He's told you that?"

"He's intimated it."

"Yes, but has he actually told you that's the type of woman he wants."

"Not exactly, but he was once almost in love with a woman, but not quite, because she wasn't a horsewoman."

"He told you that?"

Kate rolled her eyes. "Yes, Shirley."

"Well, that's just probably because he has his mind made up on what woman he thinks he should have and not what woman he'll eventually fall in love with. Go dress up. You would make a lovely couple."

"I don't think so," Kate said. "I was supposed to be married awhile back, Shirley, and I'm not over that yet."

"Oh dear. What happened?"

"He found someone else." Kate surprised herself by speaking the truth quite audibly without the threat of tears.

"So now you're free for Rafe?"

"I'm not free," Kate said. "Not free inside."

"I understand, dear. But you have to live, you know. We only come this way once. You will probably only ever meet a good man like Rafe Colson once as well. You wouldn't do badly with him."

But Kate didn't want someone she wouldn't do badly with. She would rather have no man than a man she didn't love. And she didn't want to love. It was all too painful. Although she really wondered if she hadn't loved Casey enough, and if Casey had sensed her withdrawal, and that was why he had grown away from her. That's what he had said: He'd grown away from her. Or was that just an excuse because he wasn't mature enough? He certainly wasn't as mature as Rafe. She couldn't see Casey running the farm the way Rafe did. Actually, she didn't think Casey would like it here. He preferred city living.

Oh well, she didn't have to worry about him because she didn't have him in her life anymore, she thought as she put on a long, silky light blue dress with narrow shoulder straps and a pair of thick-heeled white sandals. She arranged her hair into an upswept style and fastened a pair of silver earrings. *Wow him, Kate. Fine chance. The only way you'll ever wow Rafe Colson would be to ride a horse over the fields in the mornings the way he does.* She hadn't known Rafe did this, until on a recent morning, unable to sleep, she had heard hooves and had gone to the window. Rafe had been leaving the barn in the dusky morning light on a horse Kate wasn't sure she had seen before, a big chestnut riding horse. She had continued to watch him walk the horse up between the double fences that she had learned were called lanes. Then he had taken off over the fields, the horse and rider one, a magnificent sight.

When the doorbell rang, Kate thought it was the guests arriving early. But it was Rafe Shirley let in as Kate reached the top of the stairs. He wore a maroon shirt with a muted black pattern on it and a pair of smart black pants. She walked down to greet him.

"I came over early, thinking you might need help," he said, handing her a bottle of wine and a box of chocolates.

"Everything's under control, Rafe. But the thought was sweet." She admired his choice of wine. "This is nice. And the chocolates look delicious. Thank you very much."

"So you don't need help?"

"No. Shirley's helping, and I think I heard Alan come in."

He smiled. ''Are they acting like Mom and Pop?''

She clutched the wine and chocolates he had selected for her. ''Some days it feels that way, but it's nice to have them around.''

Fitz raced over and pawed up to Rafe, and he knelt down and nuzzled the puppy.

''He'll get hairs all over you, Rafe.''

''Don't worry. Where are the cats?''

''Hiding. They never come out when Shirley and Alan are here, only when I'm alone. But they all sleep with me at night.''

''That's sweet,'' Rafe said as he straightened, brushing down his black slacks.

He followed Kate into the sunroom, where she was having the guests congregate, and she wondered if he meant that, or if he was merely being personable this evening. She placed the chocolates and wine on a table. Was she feeling different with him as a result of her conversation with Shirley, or because her own feelings had definitely changed toward him?

''Keep them for yourself,'' he said.

Were they especially for her? The thought made her feel slightly giddy, very special, and then she scolded herself for being silly. People in business gave one another gifts like wine and chocolate all the time. That was all it was. She didn't want to be in love. It was better this way.

"I'll leave them here, then if someone wants a chocolate or we run out of wine, we can use them."

"Okay. Whatever." He settled himself down on one of the wicker sofas and stretched out his legs. "You're making this place nice, Kate."

She looked around, trying not to focus on Rafe. "I keep changing bits of furniture. But my uncle had some very valuable pieces."

"Yes, he did." Rafe laid his arm across the sofa back. "I think it's a good thing you are here carrying on the family tradition."

She met his brilliant eyes. "I'm pleased you think it's working out."

"Let's hope it does. The fun hasn't begun yet with the racing."

The doorbell rang again. Kate went away to answer it. It was her Uncle Ron and Aunt Sadie with their spouses. Everyone seemed pleased to see her, and as Kate had predicted, they couldn't hold back their curiosity. As she gave the elderly couples a tour of the house, she noticed they tried not to appear overeager about Fitz's circumstances.

"This wasn't to be expected of Fitz, you know," Sadie told Kate as she introduced Rafe and they settled down with him to chat.

"He was a gambler," Ron said and looked

around the elegant home. ‘‘But I guess he gambled on the right horses.’’

‘‘He sure did,’’ Ron’s wife said, and Sadie’s husband agreed. He had obviously been around when the Fitz problem had arisen.

‘‘Did Fitz and Nell ever have a baby?’’ Kate asked, remembering something her mother had mentioned.

‘‘We did hear something,’’ Ron told her. ‘‘But I’m not sure if it was true or not. But if he had a child, he would have left the farm to his next of kin, wouldn’t he?’’

‘‘There was no one I ever met,’’ Rafe said. ‘‘Fitz never mentioned a son or daughter.’’

‘‘Probably disowned him,’’ Sadie said a little scathingly. ‘‘He was very much the type of man who did what he wanted to do. He went his own way.’’

‘‘Isn’t that commendable?’’ Rafe remarked.

Kate passed him a glance. No one usually disputed Sadie and Ron’s opinion of Fitz.

Sadie coughed. ‘‘Yes. Well, I suppose. He obviously got rich. And he has passed the wealth back to his family. That’s commendable.’’

The doorbell rang again and Kate escaped. It was sort of fun witnessing her relative’s reaction to the farm. This time it was her parents with Joe and Kim. Everyone was really impressed with the house now that Kate’s belongings were in place.

"You're fine here, are you, Katie?" her father asked, with his arm around her shoulders.

"I love it," she told him truthfully.

Her mother smiled. "I think I could get used to this lovely house quite easily as well."

Her friends Iris and David arrived next. They had been engaged for a year now and were planning a wedding next summer. Kate had attended high school with Iris, who was slim, dark-haired and vivacious, with the perfect personality for her job with children at the community center. David was a solemn accountant, slim, handsome and quite shy at times. Iris called him a honey, and Kate believed her. He was a kind, gentle man.

Iris joined Kate in the kitchen for a private chat. "No wonder you moved here, Kate. He's *so* nice."

Kate shook her head. "I didn't move here because of him."

"No," Iris said, sniffing a dish of delicious lasagna, "but I bet he influenced your decisions."

"He influenced me all right, Iris. He runs the horses."

Iris pried herself away from the appetizing food. "Anyway, I have a message for you from Casey."

Kate's stomach turned over. She looked at Iris,

and she knew she had turned pale. Her entire body was shaking. ‘‘What?’’

‘‘Well, he says to say hi. He’s broken up with Edwina, and he regrets his decision about you.’’

‘‘Regrets, Iris? He broke up with me a month before our wedding day. Regrets?’’ Kate turned away, holding her burning forehead. ‘‘I don’t want to see him again, ever.’’

Iris put her arm around Kate’s shoulders. ‘‘All right. But I said I would ask. I *did* tell him you probably wouldn’t want to.’’

‘‘Of course I don’t want to. I never want to see him again in my life. And how dare he send you as messenger instead of calling me himself!’’

‘‘Ah, Kate. It’s difficult because I work with him.’’

‘‘I can’t help that.’’

Knowing that Casey now didn’t have Edwina as a girlfriend upset Kate more than she would have imagined. *Don’t think about him being free*, she told herself. *He’s a creep.*

Her stomach was churning so badly, Kate barely ate any of the food she had so diligently planned and prepared.

Her Uncle Ron lifted his glass and toasted Kate, saying, ‘‘I was going to do this on your wedding day, Kate, but I’ll do it for your house-warming instead. Good luck, Sweetie.’’

Tears began to drip down Kate’s cheeks, and

she quickly got up from her seat and picked up some empty plates to take into the kitchen. Someone rapidly followed her.

"Kate."

It was Rafe. She wanted to control herself, but she couldn't. She clutched the edge of the counter and began to sob. And finally it seemed everything that she had kept bottled up was bursting out of her.

"Oh Kate." Rafe put his arms around her and gently twisted her to face him.

Kate soaked his shirt with her tears. When she couldn't cry anymore, he held her, soothing her, his hand caressing the nape of her neck.

"Okay now?' he asked softly.

She nodded and moved away from him, but he didn't let her go. With his fingers, he gently removed the tears.

"Don't let that upset you."

"It's not only that." She touched the patch on his shirt where her tears dampened it. "I've ruined your shirt."

"It doesn't matter. What else happened?"

"Casey, my ex-fiancé, is a lifeguard where Iris works."

"A lifeguard?"

"Yes. Iris works at a community center, and there's a pool. That's how I met him."

"Okay. So what happened?"

"She told me he had broken up with Edwina, and he wants me back again."

Kate thought Rafe's features seemed awfully taut. "You're not thinking about it though, are you?" he demanded.

"No. I'm not."

He suddenly drew her against his chest and cradled her there.

"There's so much pain, Rafe."

He stroked her back. "I know. But it will go. Now go upstairs and fix yourself up, and I'll serve the coffee."

"You're so sweet," she told him, holding him. He was strong and sensible and terribly attractive.

"Sweet," he said with a smile as they parted. "No one's ever described me as sweet before."

"You're a kind man. That's what I mean."

Kate thought she saw him swallow hard, and then he ushered her away from the kitchen. "Fix yourself up. I'll deal with the guests."

Uncle Ron apologized when she went back into the room.

"I didn't think. I'm sorry, Katie."

"It's okay," she told him. And it probably was. She was gradually working everything out. One day she would rise from the ashes. She knew she would.

They drank their coffee with the patio door open, and then most of the guests went outside to look at the pool. Rafe sat with her and Iris and David talking about different things, and it was nice to have him beside her. Once in a while Rafe would look at Kate and smile and she smiled back, hoping he didn't mind being here as her partner. What if he was making it a duty? A duty for a jilted bride? She could still see a stain on his shirt where her tears had spilled.

Everyone gradually left, but Rafe stayed on with her. Shirley and Alan had already retired to one of the back bedrooms in the house, so Kate carried some things into the kitchen. Rafe followed her in with a couple of cups.

"The evening mainly went well," he said.

She put the tray on the counter and absently tucked her hair behind her ear. "Mainly. Thank you for coming."

"I wouldn't have missed it, Kate. Really."

"But you wanted to miss it."

"Well." He sighed. "I didn't think you were going to pay attention to the farm, and I thought you might just become interested in the social side of racing because there *is* a big social side. I think I was wrong about that, so I have to say I'm sorry for that misconception. I'm also sorry you were upset."

"I'm fine now. In fact I feel quite calm."

"It doesn't do any harm to let it all out."

"I know."

Rafe placed his hands on her shoulders and pulled her close to him. It was a bit like the first time when they sealed the partnership deal in Graeme's parking lot. Rafe lowered his head, and gave her a light kiss on the lips. But this time he didn't stop. His mouth deepened upon hers. Kate hadn't been kissed romantically since Casey. For a moment she almost pushed Rafe away in a panic, and then thought better of it. Why give up the pleasures in life because of a creep like Casey? So she placed her hands on his shoulders and moved closer to him. Besides, it was better than with Casey. Rafe's kiss sent her heart and mind spinning, and she forgot how long the kiss actually went on before they parted and stepped away from one another.

Kate held on to the edge of the counter.

Rafe raked his hair back with his fingers. "I'd better go. It's late. Do you want help with this?" His voice was husky.

She looked at the few dishes left. "No, it's fine. I'm sure we'll handle it in the morning."

"Fine. I didn't see to the horses before I came this evening."

She raised an eyebrow. "That's all you think about, horses?"

"No. It's not all," he told her. "It's not all."

She didn't know what he meant, but she let him go and stood around in the kitchen feeling sad. Then finally she began to move around and went upstairs to bed. After about ten minutes all the animals trooped upstairs and settled around her. She had expected to think about Casey, but instead she dreamed of Rafe's kiss.

Kate went downstairs on Sunday morning to discover that Shirley and Alan had cleared up all the party mess, and the house appeared spotless.

"Thank you," Kate said. "I was prepared to work all day."

"You relax today," Shirley told her. "Or go play with the horses."

"Me, play with horses?" Kate laughed, and her laughter sounded fresh and clear to her ears. The party must have been cathartic, and she felt light of heart, almost giddy, for the first time in ages.

Shirley wiped the counter clean. "You should learn to ride a horse. Get young Crystal to teach you. She has teaching certificates."

Kate smiled. "Shirley, that advice wouldn't have anything to do with what I said about Rafe preferring a horsewoman, would it?"

"A little," Shirley admitted. "But why not ride?"

"Why not?" Kate said. But she wasn't too enthralled about putting herself upon a horse in front of Rafe. She always felt she had enough to prove to him without trying to do what he did easily. Riding was second nature to Rafe. So was kissing, she thought. His kiss last night wasn't leaving her. Just thinking about his mouth upon hers made her head spin, and she wondered if it was Rafe who was making her feel so light-hearted. She also wondered if he felt the same way. What if they did fall in love?

With Fitz gamboling by her feet, Kate walked down to the barn. It was promising to be a hot, humid day, and she could feel the perspiration gather beneath her clothing. Her heart leapt when she saw Rafe standing by the barn, foot lodged on the wall. But she felt her heart squeeze shut in protection as she noticed he was talking to a woman with long raven hair and lovely features. The woman was very slim in khaki pants and an army green T-shirt. Rafe's expression was enraptured.

Fitz raced up to Rafe. Rafe picked up the dog, who began licking his face.

"A friend?" the woman asked.

"A good friend. This is Fitz. And this is Kate, Arden's niece. This is Rachel Vargis, our vet, Kate."

"Hi, Kate." Rachel shook her hand. "Pleased to meet you. Rafe's mentioned you, but we don't seem to meet."

"Well, we have now," Kate said, curbing the

jealousy. She had no right to be jealous of Rafe's attention to other women, except he had kissed her last night. Unless it had just been a comfort kiss. He probably felt sorry for her because she couldn't keep her man, and he thought a kiss might cheer her up. And all it really did was confuse her even more. The lighthearted feeling was now gone.

"Anyway, Rafe," Rachel touched his arm. "I'll get going. All the horses look fine. Just keep the bandages on Springtime for another few days."

The vet drove a blue Jeep, a similar model to Rafe's. Rafe jumped into the passenger seat to go with Rachel to open the gates. And Kate stomped into the barn. A woman couldn't trust any man. One evening he was comforting her and kissing her in her kitchen, the next morning he was flirting with the beautiful vet. She patted Talisman. "I hope I can trust you to win races and live out my uncle's dreams."

Fitz was running up and down the barn. "Come on, Fitz," she commanded. "We're going back to the house."

After she had eaten breakfast, Kate felt very restless. Maybe because the party was over. The aftermath left her in a bit of a low mood. Not to mention Rafe and Rachel. *Oh, Casey*, she thought, as she strode through the house to her uncle's study. *Why did you leave me? But I can't take you back. I really can't. You've destroyed whatever I felt.*

Once she was in the study, Kate looked at all the photographs again. This time she noticed a few with a woman in them. In some the woman had dark hair, in others she was gray-haired. The way Fitz looked at her, Kate realized it must be Nell. She picked up one of the photos and peered at it in the sunlight streaming from the window. Nell had been a lovely woman. No wonder Fitz had missed her after she died.

She replaced the photo, wondering what to do. All the family differences were really water under the bridge now, and Kate was here and she had to make the most of her farm ownership. She knew she still had a great deal to learn if she was going to help Rafe make Fitzhenry Farm operate the way it had when her uncle was around. Therefore, she spent most of the week reading. She read all about the care and temperament of race horses. She read about pulmonary hemorrhages that caused bleeding in the lungs, and that horses sometimes swallowed their tongues. She learned about the use of Lasix, the drug to stop the bleeding, and also about tongue straps. Sometimes she thought aspects of horse racing seemed pretty cruel, but she kept learning. She was in this now. There was no turning back. So much so that she would also have to get used to seeing Rafe with various women. *Forget his kisses, Kate and stick to business.* The way he had transferred his attentions from her last night to Rachel this morning was an indication he might be just a flirt.

Chapter Eight

When Kate emerged from her reading foray a few days later, she discovered the weather was even more humid than it had been on Sunday. Kate began to make use of the pool. She would take a bunch of horse books with her to the pool, cool off in the glittery water, then sit and read the books until she was hot again. Rafe had been away, racing a few of the horses during the week, but he was back by Friday when the humidity lay heavily over the entire farm.

When Kate saw Rafe come through the gate after lunch, she stood up from her lounger and picked up her towel robe. She wrapped it around her plain black swimsuit. "Hi," she said, tying the belt. "You're back?" She hadn't actually talked to him since the Sunday morning after the party, when he'd been with Rachel.

He stuck his hands into the back pockets of his jeans. "Yep. I'm back. We had a couple of wins, so I made some money for the farm operation."

"Wonderful," she told him with a big, rather forced smile.

He frowned. "What's wrong?"

"Nothing's wrong. It's just hot. Shouldn't we celebrate?"

"Let's save our celebration for Talisman's win," he said and looked rather longingly at the water.

"Do you want to swim?" Kate asked.

"I wouldn't mind," he said. "I think I deserve some time off."

"Definitely. You do." She thought of herself swimming and reading most of the week while he had been working. Although she had dealt with a little business, and the knowledge she had gained from her reading was necessary. She needn't feel guilty.

"Problem?" he asked.

He seemed to be able to read her thoughts sometimes. She shook her head hard. "No. Go get changed and swim."

While he was gone, Kate threw off her robe to display her plain black suit, and slipped into the water. She was swimming hard when Rafe returned, wearing shorts and a T-shirt.

"Demons on your tail?" he shouted.

"No. I just like swimming hard." Kate watched him strip down to black swim briefs. Casey had been a blue-eyed, blond Greek god lifeguard, a beautiful man to some women. Rafe, Kate saw, was just as hard muscled, except his muscles came from physical labor and not the gym. He was much more attractive, and she wished he wasn't.

Smoothing his hair, he walked to the edge. "Are you over the party?"

She squeezed water from her hair. "What was there to get over?"

"You know, everything."

She thought about his kiss, which every once in a while became real upon her mouth again. Then she thought about Rachel the next morning. "I'm fine," she said abruptly and began to swim again.

Behind her, Kate heard a splash and soon Rafe was swimming beside her. They swam side by side for a number of laps. He even swam well. There was nothing to fault him with, she decided as she stopped breathlessly at one end.

Rafe joined her. "Why are you so agitated?"

"I'm not agitated, Rafe. The weather is hot."

"Yeah, but it's cool in the water. What happened after the party?"

Kate glanced away from his brilliant eyes. "I don't know what you're talking about."

"If that's the case," he said, "thanks for the swim."

He left abruptly, picked up his towel and his clothes. With his towel tucked around his waist, he strode out of the gate.

Kate dipped her shoulders beneath the water. She probably had been hoping too hard when she thought the farm would eliminate her misery.

In the next week or so Kate certainly understood why they had needed more employees. Rafe, Marc and Crystal began to go away more and more. Rafe earned money, and Kate took care of the accounting side of the business. Occasionally they had to work together in Rafe's office, or he came into her office, where she set up identical systems on her computer. She could feel the partnership melding, becoming stronger. The farm was working.

When Rafe and Marc's parents came for dinner one Saturday, Rafe invited Kate to join them. It was still hot, so she dressed in white cotton slacks and a silky purple blouse. Rafe's parents were younger than she expected. His mother, Dorothy, was a small, dark-haired lady, well dressed in a linen suit. And his father, John, was slim and jovial. Rafe, Marc and Crystal had prepared one of their barbecues in the cottage courtyard. Kate was left to entertain Dorothy and John as their sons and Crystal arranged the food on a table.

"It's great you came along and gave Rafe the chance to stay here," John told her. "It's nice to have both of our sons close to home now."

Kate smiled. "I couldn't do this without Rafe. He has so much knowledge about horses."

Dorothy leaned forward. "But he told me he couldn't have done it without you, so I'm sure you're working at this equally."

Kate was pleased she had heard that news from Rafe's mother because sometimes she felt very helpless and almost useless in the operation of the horse business. "Maybe. But I would like to be able to ride a horse," she said.

Crystal was carrying out plates. "I'll teach you, Kate. After I've done the stalls each morning, we'll have lessons. How's that?"

Shirley had suggested this, and now Kate agreed. Riding the horses was the only way she was going to become more involved with them.

For all her trepidation Kate enjoyed the evening with the Colsons, and when everyone left to go home, Crystal reminded her of their lessons.

"You're going to learn to ride?" Rafe asked as he walked her across the meadow in the warm evening air.

"Yes, I am. I feel useless otherwise."

"Kate. That's not true. You've been the catalyst behind this entire enterprise."

"No, I haven't, Rafe. You do most of the

work. I've read some books and paid a few bills, but I don't feel as if I pull my weight. If I learn to ride, I'll learn more about the temperament of horses."

"As long as you're not doing it to prove something."

Kate glanced at him. He seemed to catch on to all her motives. "No. Not really."

"That's good."

They reached the door, and Kate watched Rafe stride away. No more kisses, she thought, which was really the way it should be between them.

Crystal was a very patient teacher. Kate's first lessons were learning everything there was to know about the horse's body parts and the tack she would be using to ride. On her third lesson, she actually had to mount the horse. Being so high up made her feel quite giddy and sick for a while.

"You'll be okay," Crystal said, leading the horse to the paddock. "Lottie won't hurt you. She's a very calm riding horse."

Kate grinned gingerly down at her as she clutched the reins. "If you say so."

Kate ended up with aching limbs, so she wasn't in very good shape for Talisman's first race at Saratoga. As Kate had never been to a racetrack before, she wasn't sure what to do. She had to ask Rafe.

"Dress up," he said. "Owners always dress up. Do you have a hat?"

"No, I don't. Unless you count this." She touched the baseball cap she wore.

He smiled. "No, I don't think so. It might be a good idea if you bought a straw hat, and then you can use it for the season."

"All right. I'll do that."

On Saturday there was a televised race, and Rafe called her into the cottage to watch. Kate sat down on one of the chairs in front of the set and began to doubt her ability to go on with this. She couldn't see herself looking like those well-dressed, well-bred people in the stands.

"All you have to do is be there, Kate," Rafe said softly. As usual it seemed as if he tuned into her doubts.

On the day of Talisman's race, Kate dressed in a very pale green linen suit, along with a big straw hat, to which she added a green ribbon. Rafe wore a suit, reminding her of the day they had signed the papers.

Rafe escorted her along the shedrow to the Fitzhenry Farm barn. He introduced Kate as Fitz's niece. It seemed everyone knew a story about her uncle and respected the farm's reputation. However, Kate noticed they appeared intent on their mission with their horses, and it really hit home to Kate that racing was indeed a serious business. A make-or-break business for most people, if they weren't independently rich, and even if they were very wealthy, they likely had so much investment tied up in a stable that their horses couldn't lose, or get injured. There was so much to worry about, she still wondered if it was all worth the effort. But she changed her mind when she saw Talisman, as bright as ever, groomed by Crystal until his black mane was fluffy, his tail neatly braided partway down and brushed full at the end. Kate's anxiety turned to excitement. He stood proud, wanting to race. For Uncle Fitz. For Rafe. For herself.

Standing with Rafe in the ring with other men and women in fashionable clothes, Kate watched the numbered horses being led around by the grooms. Jockeys, all of similar height and size to theirs, whose name was Trent Kane, wore colorful silk shirts and helmets and strode around brandishing riding sticks.

Brilliant in the magenta-and-white silks of Fitzhenry Farm, Trent mounted Talisman. Trent was a mild-mannered, slow talking man, and Talisman usually responded to his gentle hands. Today Talisman restlessly taunted the lead pony as they joined the rest of the field at the gate. Kate thought he seemed ready to race. It was almost as if the horse knew what he was going to do.

Later, sitting beside Rafe above the track, Kate

trembled with nervousness. She whispered *good luck* to Rafe, but he merely nodded. She wished he would show more emotion. Kate bit into her lip as she watched the horses being loaded into the gate.

They're off.

The patrons in the seats in front rose, and Kate stood up to peer around their shoulders. Number Seven, like to Sprint, led coming out of the gate. She screamed, "Come on, Talisman! Come on, Talisman!" She saw on the infield board number that Seven was still leading as the horses raced along the backstretch. Talisman led coming along the straight until a chestnut horse on Talisman's right moved up and passed Talisman at the finish by a length. Like to Sprint had won its first race. Talisman hadn't.

Kate sat down with a thump. He hadn't won, even if he had made some money for the farm for second place. But money wasn't the point. She had been geared up for Talisman to win. Rafe's training expertise all pointed to a win. Rafe had pretty well assured her that he would win.

She glanced at Rafe, and he didn't meet her gaze. No, he couldn't, could he? She'd put all her trust in him and he'd let her down. His training had come up short on this race. This was a terrible situation. Talisman had to win. She had promised her uncle many times in her head that this would be the case.

"What's the matter?" Rafe asked as they returned to the barn to see Talisman.

"He didn't win."

"Them's the breaks."

She glanced at him. "That's all you can say?"

"There's only one winner in each race. Talisman didn't go the distance this race. Next race."

"Promise?"

"I'm not promising anything in such a fragile business, Kate."

"But you did think he was better?"

He touched her waist to guide her around another horse and groom. "He *is* better. Give him a chance."

Talisman was home the next day being pampered in his stall. Kate was up early and down to the barn. Rafe led her into his office and slotted a video of the race into a VCR on the TV set. Watching the race again was equally as exciting, and just as disappointing as Like to Sprint overtook Talisman at the finish. Kate had thought about her reaction to Talisman's loss overnight, and she had decided that she still had faith in Rafe. There would be a next time.

After Talisman's first race, Kate became fully aware of the elite circle she had now joined as owner of Fitzhenry Farm, when she was inundated by invitations from people she had met at the track. She came to the conclusion that her uncle had been very well thought of.

Louise Maxwell even invited her to a party one Saturday evening. Louise told her that Rafe was also invited and had already accepted. Kate mentioned the party to Rafe the next day after Talisman's workout.

She followed him around as he shifted tack onto shelves. In the warm weather he always wore a T-shirt or short-sleeved shirt, and she enjoyed watching his muscles flex as he worked, remembering the day in the pool. He'd been extremely cool to her since that day, and she didn't really know why, except there seemed to be a tension between them since her party. At first she thought it was in her own mind because of Rachel, but now she was sure it was emanating from Rafe as well. "I didn't think you liked parties," she said.

"It's difficult to say no to Louise," he said. "Although her dos are the worst. They're all about one-upmanship. Are you going?"

"I said I would. I mean I can't really afford not to be neighborly."

"True. Shall we go together?"

Kate's heart leapt, and she wished it hadn't. "You mean as business partners?"

He raised an eyebrow at her. "What else is there between us, Kate?"

She shrugged. The tension *was* coming from him as well, and she wondered if he regretted kissing her at the party and was pushing her away. "Nothing, I guess."

"Well, then you have to admit it's silly to take two vehicles just to drive next door. We can go in your car as the Jeep is more fit for horses. So you say."

Ah, that was his reasoning. Why take two vehicles when one would do? Why bother to clean out his vehicle when he could go in hers? She lifted her chin, almost convinced to turn him down, but she didn't. "Well, it is messy, Rafe. All right. I'm not taking anyone else with me."

He dumped some tack hard down onto a table. He wasn't looking at her. "Who would you take?" His voice was harsh.

It infuriated Kate that he thought she couldn't get a date. She wished she had never told him about Casey. "I don't know," she said.

He looked down at the tack he had dumped. "You say that as if you want someone. I thought you were convinced you were never going to fall in love again?"

She noticed the way his shirt stretched over his muscular back, and she had to fight with herself not to reach out and touch him. "I'm not—going to fall in love again, but I might need a date once in a while. You know, for events like Louise's party.''

Rafe moved away from her, picked up a saddle and heaved it upon a shelf with more force than necessary. ''Have we decided we will go together?''

''Okay. Fine''

He turned around, and she thought he looked weary. ''That's what I suggested in the first place, Kate. Why go through a song and dance about it?''

He made her feel like a fool. She adjusted her baseball cap over her long fall of hair. ''I don't know, why?'' But she did. Hurt and pain over Casey was dull now, and the feelings were being replaced by feelings for Rafe. Strong feelings. Emotions much more erratic than anything she had ever felt for Casey. She was beginning to see that she might have made a huge mistake by marrying Casey. He might have done her a big favor by dumping her. Hadn't everyone told her that?

Rafe watched her. ''It's settled. We go together.''

''Yes.'' Kate left then, otherwise she had a feeling they might have had an argument. She wasn't sure what was going on between them. Or was it just her stronger feelings for Rafe manifesting a situation that didn't exist?

Knowing the circle Louise Maxwell moved in, Kate really fussed with what she would wear to the party. She denied to herself that her fussing had anything to do with Rafe. But she knew it had all to do with him, as with an almost tearful frustration she found nothing satisfactory in her wardrobe. Consequently, she drove into Ellis Corners, where she discovered a little store with a minimum of clothing in stock, but all beautiful designs. That was where she found the white, extremely lightweight, velvet dress. Long-sleeved, low necked and very svelte, it flowed down to a spot above her ankles. She purchased some high-heeled leather sandals to accompany it and a new evening bag.

After Kate dressed in the new dress, for a little extra zap she curled her hair and coiled it upon her head. She had discovered diamond earrings in a box in one of the bedrooms and she wore those, leaving her throat bare. She heard the front doorbell ring. Knowing it was Rafe, she picked up her new bag and went down to greet him.

He wore a black evening suit, a silk shirt and a black silk bow tie. Inhaling his subtle after-shave, Kate felt tongue-tied. He was so different dressed up like this. A stranger? She couldn't believe she had transferred her pain for Casey to Rafe, another man she might never have.

"Hi," she said, endeavoring to sound normal.

"Hi." He seemed amused as his gaze appraised her. "You look very lovely."

"So do you—look handsome, that is."

He grinned. "I'm pleased you clarified that. Are you ready to leave?"

She handed him her car keys and felt the electric brush of his fingers upon hers. He felt different to her now that she was falling in love with him.

It was a still, warm evening, and the pool courtyard at the Maxwell's house was crowded with guests. Dinner was going to be a buffet, but there were little hot snacks circulating with the drinks.

Kate noticed that Louise glued herself to Rafe's side, and she realized that she hadn't been wrong on that first visit, Louise really did like him, despite having a handsome young husband of her own. Kate felt that this was sheer greed. She eased up closer to him.

"Kate," he said, looking relieved and putting his arm around her waist. "Do you think we should mingle?"

"Definitely." Kate glanced at Louise. "Louise has so many interesting-looking guests."

Louise's smile seemed forced. "Of course you must meet everyone. I'll see you later, Rafe."

"I'll see you later, Rafe," Kate mocked. "She didn't even see me."

"She saw you," he said, laughing. "Thanks for saving me." He squeezed her waist but didn't withdraw his arm.

"I *did* think Louise had a crush on you when I visited her the first time, and she asked about you."

He made a face. "Maybe your act will discourage her."

"You don't like her?"

His arm drew her even closer, and he lowered his head close to hers. "It's not a case of not liking her. She's married. I have strict guidelines."

His closeness, his subtle aftershave, everything about him, made her heart beat fast. "Which are?" she asked breathlessly.

"No married women."

"And women who are only interested in horses?" Kate added.

He laughed. "Where did you get that idea?"

"You told me that first day when you were fixing my tire."

His eyebrows met in a frown. "I never said that, did I?"

"Not exactly, but you mentioned that you hadn't loved Jennifer because she didn't share your passion for horses."

"I'm not sure about that, Kate. I was a lot younger. I wasn't ready for love."

"How do you know when you are ready for love?"

"I think you just know. My parents always told me that. Did you know with, um, whatshis-name?"

"Casey?" Kate spoke his name evenly, without a change of tone. "I thought I did."

"Are you over him now?"

"I don't know quite, but I'm not so hung up. I don't cry myself to sleep anymore. I think about other things, like the horses and the business and learning to ride." *And you.*

He moved her with his arm, so she was facing him. "That's good news, Kate. It was horrible to see you so sad. To know you were so sad. Some evenings I wanted to come over and comfort you."

She gazed into his eyes. He didn't remove his glance from her face.

"I did. I thought of poor little you over in that big house alone. Then you got the animals, and I didn't worry quite so much."

That he had actually worried about her made her heart feel warm and alive. "Oh, Rafe."

He kissed her nose. "Come on. Smile. Let's go do that circulating."

They soon found themselves in the midst of a crowd of people, all chatting about horses. Kate listened, interested in their talk about breeding, until dinner was announced. The buffet was hot chicken and beef, and all kinds of salads. Dessert was either plump strawberries dipped in chocolate, or white chocolate mousse. Rafe and Kate dipped a lot of strawberries in chocolate.

"You like chocolate?" she asked, patting her stomach, thinking she had to quit this indulgence before she got sick.

He swallowed another strawberry. "I love chocolate. Did you finish those ones I left you?"

"I limit myself to one each evening."

He chuckled. "But tonight you didn't limit yourself. Have you had enough now?

"Do I look green?" she asked.

He scrutinized her. "No. Not exactly green. Maybe a little pale, though."

She touched her cheek with her fingertips. "Do I really look pale?"

"Yes. I think some exercise is required. Do you want to dance?"

Music played from two speakers, and some couples circled in the courtyard by the pool. "All right," she said as he took hold of her elbow.

"I'm warning you, I'm not the greatest dancer in the world, Kate."

Maybe dancing was something she would be better at, she thought as Rafe opened the buttons on his suit jacket and put his arms around her. Kate pressed her palm against his chest, feeling the warmth and vitality of his body. She heard him draw in a breath, and she looked up at him. He leaned down and brushed her mouth with his, and then he tucked her head against his shoulder. Kate closed her eyes, realizing that this place, in Rafe's arms, was where she always wanted to be.

They danced until the music stopped and then went to look for cool drinks. Kate wondered if she was hogging Rafe's attention this evening. Maybe he had other friends here he wanted to be with. She decided to go and find a powder room and let him free for a while. She needed to think about Rafe. She was in love with him. She couldn't think of any other feeling her emotions resembled. But it wasn't an easy love, like the one she had shared with Casey. She yearned for Rafe in a way she had never yearned for Casey. But there was a similarity; she probably would never have Rafe either.

Chapter Nine

Kate regretted her decision to leave Rafe alone as soon as she returned and saw him standing near a little fountain talking to Louise. Disappointed, Kate found a seat somewhere quiet under an umbrella and watched Rafe circulate among the guests without her. Why had she left him alone? Now he looked perfectly happy by himself. He had probably stuck with her for the first half of the party because he felt he was obliged to, danced with her to please her, kissed her because that's maybe what she had communicated she wanted. Did he know she was halfway in love with him? And would he take advantage of that?

She realized she didn't really know him. Oh yes, she knew the horseman Rafe. The man who worked in the barn, trained horses and was diligent in the business workings of the farm. But she didn't know Rafe the man very well. She didn't know about his relationships with other women, other than Jennifer, whom he hadn't truly loved. But he must have been in love at some time to have known he wasn't in love with Jennifer. She saw him strolling over to her and sighed deeply to stop her heartbeat from quickening.

"Why do you look so sad at a party?" Rafe asked, sitting across from her and stretching out his legs. He fiddled with the bow tie, loosening it rakishly.

"I'm fine," she said. "Are you having fun yet?"

He shrugged his shoulders. "I've met a few people I haven't seen for a while. I was waiting for you to come back to me."

She missed meeting his eyes. "I thought you would be better alone for a while."

"Whatever."

She let out a deep sigh.

"Kate?" He leaned forward, hands resting on his knees. "Are you okay?"

She met his gaze then. He was close, too close. She could see the fine pores of his skin. "I'm fine, Rafe."

"You look worn out. Do you want to go home now?"

Home. Rafe in his box in the cottage. Kate in her box in the house. "Do you?"

"Yeah. We have early mornings with the horses."

Of course they couldn't forget the early mornings with the horses. But that was an uncharitable thought. They had responsibilities. Rafe took his seriously, she should be pleased he was that type of person. "All right," she agreed and stood up, smoothing her dress.

He also stood up and took hold of her hand. She closed her eyes tightly for a second. When they held hands, everything felt so right.

They drove home. Kate sat beside Rafe, feeling as if she were aching inside. This was ridiculous, she thought. She had just recovered from one love to be attacked by another. What was wrong with her? Did she enjoy suffering?

After summoning Alan to open the gate, Rafe climbed into her car beside her and drove through the gates.

"Weren't we going to get something modern to open the gates with?" she asked irritably.

"Yes, we were. I thought you were going to check into it?"

"I forgot, but I will."

"Great." He parked her car by the front door. "I'll see you in," he said, leaving the car and moving to open her door before she had a chance to open it herself. He took hold of her hand and helped her from the seat.

"Thank you," she told him, her fingers clutching his, and then she sort of stumbled on the gravel and she was in his arms.

His kiss was much more passionate than any of the others. This one made Kate feel special, loved, needed, wanted, all the things she desired Rafe to make her feel. She kissed him back without thinking that she was showing him how much she liked him, how much she longed for him. When he lifted his mouth from hers, it was with obvious reluctance, and she could see he was as unsteady on his feet as she was herself.

"Your front door key?" he asked and put out his hand.

She fumbled in her bag and gave it to him. He went up the steps two at a time and opened the front door for her. She came up beside him.

"Give it time, Kate," he said. "Don't rush things. I'll see you tomorrow."

"Do you want to come through the house? It's quicker."

"No," he said. "I need a walk."

She heard his footsteps on the pathway, remembering her first day here, following him around the house, following him to the barn. She had witnessed his intensity, his honesty. He'd come clean with her. He had wanted to stay here.

Now he kissed her as if he wanted her but said don't rush things, and she had to believe him and to know he was right. She couldn't be rushed. Her heart was still far too fragile.

Therefore, Kate kept her days busy. She ordered the automatic gate opener and supervised the installation. Now all they needed were remote controls from their vehicles to let them into the gates and close them behind them. She swam on warm days, read more books and took more horse riding lessons from Crystal. She found she really enjoyed riding and some days even took out a horse alone.

Rafe caught her returning one day. She thought he was at the track.

''Any luck?'' she asked him, dismounting in what she hoped was an elegant fashion.

''No wins,'' he said. ''Not even a show or place.'' He nodded toward Lottie. ''You're doing well?''

Kate patted Lottie's strong neck. ''Not bad. She's easy to handle.''

''Do you want to ride with me tomorrow morning?'' he asked.

''I can't gallop like you.'' She spoke quickly before she had time to think. Now he might guess she had watched him in the mornings. She added hurriedly, ''I saw you one morning, riding, you know, over the fields.''

Rafe chuckled. "I guessed you had. No one's asking you to gallop. We'll just walk if you want. Tomorrow?"

"Sure," she told him and wondered if she was eager to become the horsewoman he desired in his life.

Kate made sure she was up early in the morning and had Lottie saddled and ready before Rafe made an appearance. He wore jeans and a long-sleeved shirt.

"How are you doing?" he asked, as he saddled his own horse, the big chestnut, Taurus.

"Fine. I'm ready."

"You look nervous."

Kate pretended she wasn't. She had ridden with Crystal. She had ridden with Marc watching. Rafe had seen her return yesterday, but she had never been with him on a horse for any length of time. She was more than nervous. She was anxiety-ridden. Expert horsemanship was so important to Rafe. It was almost as if he measured a person's worth by her equine expertise.

After they had led their horses through the lanes, they mounted and slowly walked along the pathway that crossed the hills. The cooler morning air was wonderful after the heat they had experienced lately, and Kate breathed deeply.

"Nice, huh?" Rafe asked, riding so casually, as if he had been born melded to a horse.

"Lovely," she told him, pleased that Lottie was a gentle soul.

"You're doing well. I won't let anything go wrong."

"Nothing will go wrong," she said irritably. "I know what I'm doing."

"I realize that, but . . ."

She cut him off. "But nothing, Rafe. Just because I wasn't born riding a horse like you, doesn't mean to say I can't learn."

"I never said you couldn't."

She glared at him and touched the reins. "I'm going to trot."

"Watch it."

Luckily, Lottie didn't take off to her coaxing, and a trot was all Kate got out of the horse. When she circled back to Rafe, he was sitting on top of Taurus trying not to smile.

"You look good. You have an excellent seat. Don't overdo it, though."

They went on a little farther and circled back to the barn. Kate told Rafe to go for his normal ride, and he did, taking off across the fields as he did every morning. She wondered, as she brushed Lottie down, if she would ever be able to join him.

Talisman's second race fell on a cloudier humid day. Kate wore a black dress and her big straw hat with a white ribbon. Her feelings were no less intense than the first time Talisman raced. Judged by his initial performance, Talisman was favored to at least place. Which he did. He came second. *Again.*

Kate was terribly disappointed. She wanted Talisman to win his first race, not only because the winning purse was an amount they could use to help pay for the upkeep of the farm, but because she was impatient for Talisman to win. If he didn't win, Uncle Fitz's dreams weren't going to be realized. None of their dreams were going to be realized.

Kate returned to the farm feeling very low. Rafe was worried about Talisman's right hind leg, and he phoned Rachel as soon as they arrived home. Rachel came at once in her blue Jeep.

Kate watched her in the barn, checking out Talisman's leg, while Rafe tried to hold the horse still. Rachel wore a pair of black-framed glasses when she worked, and Kate thought she was beautiful. Smart, beautiful, horsey—every attribute that would be perfect for Rafe. Rafe walked Rachel to her vehicle when she left, and Kate wondered if he worried about her driving at night. While they were gone, Kate leaned over Talisman's stall, and the horse met her gaze.

"You're beautiful as well, Talisman. You're a winner. Prove it."

Rafe came up behind her. "I suppose you're mad at me?"

Kate turned to look at him. In the dim light of the barn, his features appeared grim. "I'm not mad at you in particular, Rafe, but second twice in a row is really upsetting."

He dug his hands into the back pockets of his jeans. "It's better than losing entirely."

"Sure it is. But there might be a reason."

"His leg was bothering him today."

"But not the first time. Maybe we should change Trent. Maybe he's too heavy or something. I was reading about the way jockeys have to diet and use a hotbox to sweat off their weight. Trent might not be fit."

"Trent's fine. He made his weight for the race."

"Then maybe you're not training Talisman as well as you should." She wished she hadn't had to say that. She had witnessed the long hours he put in working.

Rafe's shoulders stiffened. His usually glittering eyes were pale, like stones. "You really think that?"

"I don't know because I'm really not that well equipped to know. All I've done is read some books and watched what you do every morning. But he needs a win, Rafe. Otherwise all this is pointless. Uncle Fitz would say the same things to you, Rafe. It's not just me.''

He moved in closer. ''And I would answer him the same way. Horses need time and patience. The final analysis is, we're dealing with animals, and not all animals are winners.''

''But Talisman is a winner. You've told me that. Fitz believed that. I believe it. When I see Talisman against the other horses, I know he has the potential to be great. You know it as well, Rafe, otherwise you wouldn't have taken this chance with me.''

''True, but he's still pretty young and inexperienced, and we don't want to run him too hard and ruin him. I've told you that.''

''I understand, but we're not running him too hard. Are we?''

''Not on my schedule, we're not. Do you want to race him more?''

Kate straightened and brushed back a lock of hair with her hand. ''No. You do what you see fit. I guess I'm impatient. I thought things would be different.''

''I didn't. He was late starting this season because of Fitz's death. I, too, hoped for a win the first time out. I've got a financial stake in this as well, Kate. I'm not your employee, I'm your partner. You seem to have forgotten that.''

He turned around and walked out of the barn,

and left her shaken. She *had* forgotten it. She was acting like a prima donna. She wanted to run after him but didn't think it was quite the moment to begin apologizing. They both had to cool down. And, she remembered, this was strictly a business arrangement; all their kisses drifted away, like balloons caught in a slow breeze.

In the morning Kate went down to see how Talisman was. Rachel had been in to tend to his leg, and Rafe wasn't there. He had gone to visit his parents for the day and left Marc in charge.

"He seemed disappointed about Talisman," Marc told her.

"We both are," she said.

"Don't blame Rafe though, Kate. It's not his fault. Other horses are better on certain days. Track conditions, all sorts of things contribute to wins and losses."

"I know. But I think I did blame Rafe."

"No wonder he looked like thunder this morning and decided to take the day off."

Rafe didn't return until very late, and Kate spent the night tossing and turning until the animals in her bed all trooped away one by one. She went to the barn early and found him there fussing over Talisman with Rachel.

"A little joint inflammation," Rafe told Kate. "Don't worry."

Don't worry? Everything Rafe had ever

warned her about came back to haunt Kate. Was Talisman doomed? Was Uncle Fitz's dream no longer feasible? "Can we race him again this year?"

"Oh yes," Rachel said, straightening and removing her glasses at the same time. "But I would give him a few weeks to a month off. One more race might be it."

"We'll only have to scratch one race and leave him entered for the last one," Rafe said. "No problem."

Rafe took other horses to the track to race. Sometimes Kate went along. Most times the stayed behind. She swam, she rode and she worked on the business side of the racing. She loved the farm and the animals; She loved the life. But there were drawbacks—with Talisman's leg problem, Rachel was here every day.

Yesterday Kate saw her go into Rafe's cottage about lunchtime. She imagined them sitting at the little table sharing one of his meals the way she had.

The next day she needed to get away for a while, so she drove to the city to visit her parents.

"How's Rafe?" they asked.

She said. "He's fine. Just fine."

But it seemed to her that since Talisman's two losses, Rafe had erected a huge barrier between them. Or had he noticed she was in love with him by her kisses the night of Louise's party, and he wanted to put a stop to that? Or was it Rachel?

Kate looked out her window before she went to bed that night. The lights in the cottage glowed yellow. She saw Marc and Crystal leave the cottage. They weren't alone. There was another woman with them. Someone tall and willowy with very long raven-dark hair. She wore a long skirt and brief top, not vet's attire.

Kate saw Rafe talk to Rachel, then Rachel laughed. He leaned negligently against the doorway, wearing his khaki pants and white shirt, and waved Marc's truck away as they left.

The scene remained with Kate all through the next day as she worked around the house. She finally got up nerve to go down to the barn and face Rafe. She thought he seemed more relaxed and smiled at her. Probably because he could fall in love with Rachel. Jennifer had been training to be a doctor and was not quite perfect, but Rachel was a horse doctor, absolutely spot-on perfect. Kate felt so miserable, much more miserable than she had over Casey. How was she going to go on? What if Rafe decided to marry Rachel and bring her to the cottage to live? What if they had little Rafes and Rachels running around the farm? Kate saw herself as a sort of aunt figure. Even more so because she had heard a rumor that Marc and Crystal might get married next summer.

Rafe snapped his fingers at her. "What's the matter?"

"Oh. Nothing," she fibbed.

"I just told you that Talisman has been given a clean bill of health."

"By Rachel?"

"Naturally, she's the vet." He moved around restlessly, then shifted his shoulders inside his blue checked shirt. "You've been withdrawn lately, Kate."

She didn't meet his eyes. "Me? What about you? You've been cool."

"It's been worrying with Talisman not winning and then having an injury."

"Maybe that's why I've been withdrawn. I'm worried as well. But he's going to win this time," she said. "I know it."

For Talisman's last race, Kate wore a new suit with a flowing black skirt, fitted jacket with white belt and lapels, and a white wide-brimmed hat with a black ribbon. This race was a stakes race. A win from this race, and Talisman's career could take off next year. Now she understood the shortness of a horse's running years. They were all racing against time.

When Rafe met her, Kate thought they matched because Rafe looked wonderful but distant in a black suit, white shirt and silver tie. "How's Talisman?" she asked.

''Excellent shape, but you still have to cross everything.''

Kate dined with Rafe in a track restaurant. She was the new owner of Fitzhenry Farm, whose horse was entered in a prestigious race, and everyone accepted her without question as Fitz's niece; She was sure that if she'd just been a casual owner of the farm, she wouldn't have gained such instant respect.

When the time came for Talisman's race, she walked into the paddock to wish Trent luck.

Rafe was interviewed by various TV networks, and he said he thought Talisman was now ready to prove himself. They even asked Kate how she felt about the outcome. ''Positive,'' she said with a smile, holding on to her big hat in the frisky breeze. ''Absolutely positive.''

Kate sure hoped she spoke the truth on TV. If Talisman succeeded today, it would mean added prestige for the farm and the continuation of the Fitzhenry name for her uncle. She was now sure that was the reason he had left her the farm in the first place.

Kate returned to her seat with Rafe to watch to watch the race. The man beside her handed her a pair of binoculars. ''Thank you.''

He was dressed in a cream suit and had curly blond hair. He was handsome. Kate looked at Rafe to see him eyeing the other man.

He frowned. "Your type?"

"He has binoculars."

Rafe reached in his pocket and pulled out a mini pair. "You could have had these."

"Aren't you going to use those?"

"What do you think I've got around my neck?"

There was a large pair of binoculars hanging from a leather strap. "I thought it was a camera. Besides," she said, and she knew it was an intentional dig to get a rise out of Rafe. "He's a bit like Casey."

"Was he a blond Adonis?"

"Yes. A lifeguard, I told you."

"He didn't guard *your* life, did he?"

Kate bowed her head. "No, he didn't."

"Then give the guy back his binoculars, Kate, and use mine."

She did as he told her and took his mini binoculars for herself. She focused on the starting gate. Talisman was on the outside, Trent holding his energy back. Talisman really wanted to race today. It was evident by the way the horse pranced when he walked. They were in the gate. Kate suddenly felt excitement grip her. This was her livelihood now. If Talisman didn't do well, she could lose, not quite everything, but a great deal. Including the silent deal she had made with her uncle. She held her breath.

They're off.

Her heart pounded.

Talisman remained back by a number of lengths. *Oh, Talisman, come on. Come on. Come on.* Trent moved him forward. Three lengths behind third place. Two lengths behind. He was in second place now coming around the front stretch. *Talisman. Win.* Horse and rider suddenly squirted out from between the other horses; Talisman a gray streak of pounding hooves, his jockey riding high, bearing the colors of Fitzhenry Farm as they crossed the finish.

Kate let out a huge yelp, and she turned to Rafe, throwing her arms around him and planting kisses all over his face. "We did it. We did it, Rafe."

Very carefully he removed her arms from around his neck and placed them by her side.

"Take it easy," he said coolly. "It's only a win."

"A big win," she reiterated. Her face was hot with embarrassment. Why had she flung herself at him so enthusiastically?

"One of many. We hope." He touched her elbow impersonally. "Come on. We'll be wanted in the winner's circle."

Kate stood beside Rafe and Trent, Talisman was blanketed with a garland of flowers, and she was presented with the winner's silver cup. Yet really, what had she done to deserve this? It was Rafe who had trained the horse, Rachel who had nursed him and Marc who had exercised him each morning, pushing Talisman's limits. Uncle Fitz had nurtured the farm into a success and left it to Kate.

She said to the media, "He's a great horse. My Uncle Fitz believed in him. Rafe and I just continued with my uncle's dream."

Kate hugged Talisman before Crystal took him away. After all, they congratulated the humans when it was Talisman who had done all the work.

In the morning the phone started buzzing early with congratulations on Talisman's win. Magazines asked for interviews, and newspapers phoned for comments. From now on, Kate decided, sitting at her uncle's desk in the study, she was going to put her whole heart into the horse farm and forget about being in love with any man.

Kate put the phone back on the hook and swung back and forth in the chair, her gaze resting on the trophy she had now added to Fitz's. Next year will be even better, she promised her uncle's photograph. Next year I will know what I'm doing.

She placed her hand on the pile of Fitz's family albums that she hadn't given herself time to really look at yet. She had been meaning to go through these albums for a long time. She should have done it when she first came to the farm. It wasn't even a year, and it seemed as if she'd lived at Fitzhenry Farm forever.

She could barely remember a time she hadn't heard of the tracks at Saratoga and Belmont. Or a time before she learned about hocks, pasterns, chestnuts, fetlocks, coronets and cannon bones. Before breezing and bullet workouts. Before oaks races, claiming races, allowance races, stakes races, the Preakness, the Distaff, the Arlington Mile. Before turf and dirt tracks, fast tracks and yielding tracks. Before apprentice jocks or bug boys, silks and caliente helmets. Before sires, dams, broodmares and stud fees.

It was as if there had never been a time before she'd heard of the great horses: Northern Dancer, Seattle Slew, Secretariat, Sir Ivor, or Man o'War. Before handicapping, daily doubles, exactas, odds-on, win, place, show, even money, in the money and the winning purse. Before furlongs, miles, starts and straights and backstretches. Before shedrows and hot walking and exercise riding and hands on and riders up. Before Rafe. *Especially before Rafe.*

Her heart feeling heavy, Kate opened one of the albums and looked at Fitz's photos of horses. She understood the creatures more now. She turned a page, and a small black-and-white photo fell out. It was Fitz and dark-haired Nell with a baby. So Fitz *did* have a baby. So what happened to the child? Eagerly, she turned the photograph over and saw written on the back in Fitz's scratchy writing: *Katherine Nell.*

He had a baby daughter, and he'd called her Katherine. After his mother? Kate believed that to be true. She was also named after her grandmother. Then where was Katherine now? Why hadn't she inherited the farm? The answer came in an obituary further on: *Katherine Nell Fitzhenry, eight months, three days . . .*

Kate contemplated Arden Fitzhenry with his shock of silver hair, bright eyes and the appearance of a man who knew what he wanted from life. She felt very sorry she had never met him. Yet through Talisman and Rafe, she felt she knew him.

She was about to close the album and begin on another when she realized there was something else in the book. Stuck in the pages was a brittle yellow birth announcement. It was *her* birth announcement.

Oh, Uncle Fitz, she thought sadly. *I would have loved you, I'm sure. I was your Katherine. If she hadn't died, she would have inherited the farm, but instead, you gave it to me. You knew.* She gazed into her uncle's eyes in his photograph. *You knew I would come here and love it the way you loved it. Did you hope that Rafe and I would get together? Well, I might have to disappoint you there. It doesn't look like it will ever happen.*

Chapter Ten

The racing season began to wind down. Rafe had a number of wins with the other horses that would set them up financially for the winter. Kate really wondered how the winter out here on the farm would pass for her. She knew the horses still had to be attended to. Rafe had told her that horses love the cold and the snow. She was sure she would survive. If she hadn't fallen in love with Rafe, her life would be complete. But she felt he was even further from her world now. Since Talisman's last race, when he had dismissed her kisses and hug, he had acted as if he didn't really want her near him.

Still, they did have their business relationship. Kate understood now that she couldn't put all her eggs in one basket with Talisman. And after discovering just how financially fruitful a major race win could be, she was eager to acquire more stock for Rafe to train. At a neighboring breeding farm, she fell in love with a little chestnut colt yearling that looked full of life. Its pedigree, like Talisman's traced back to a famous horse. Kate named it Golden Wing and they shipped it to Fitzhenry Farm.

On the way home in his Jeep, she asked Rafe, "Are you pleased about Golden Wing?"

"He's got potential."

His voice was so even, so cool, that Kate shivered, feeling like a hot summer day was suddenly covered by an icy blanket of snow. Kate didn't really know what was wrong, but she did wonder if Rafe had fallen in love with Rachel.

Still, she wanted to at least be his friend. "I discovered why Fitz left me the farm, Rafe."

He glanced sideways. She thought he appeared interested, so she went on to explain about the obituary and her birth announcement in Fitz's albums.

"Well, that might be what it was all about. I never knew they had a baby. Long before my time."

"Exactly. But it explains why I inherited the farm."

"Yeah," he said and she thought he suddenly seemed very weary.

Kate drew in a breath and let it out slowly. She shouldn't ask this. "What is it?"

He thumped the steering wheel with the palm of his hand. "What's what, Kate?"

"Your distant attitude since Talisman won."

He gave her a long look. "Figure it out, Kate. Just figure it out."

Rachel was at the farm when they arrived home, and Kate knew what he meant. He had fallen in love with the perfect vet. She went into the house and shut her doors tightly, feeling as if her heart was going to break. She must enjoy this, she told herself, otherwise she wouldn't keep falling in love with men who didn't love her.

In the morning Kate felt very rough. A headache crept around her temples, and her heart was heavy. It was a crisp, sunny October day, so she decided to saddle Lottie and go for a ride. She was quite adept at cantering now. She rode carefully as she always did, feeling the breeze blow her hair and cool her face until it was rosy. When she returned to the barn, she dismounted and tethered Lottie outside for her brush down.

Rafe strode out of the barn. "You were up early, Kate?"

"Yes. I couldn't sleep very well. Have you had your ride yet?"

"I didn't feel like it this morning. I was hoping to see you, though. Samantha has invited you to a Halloween Ghost Ride on Friday evening. I'm going, and so are Marc and Crystal. We'll make up a foursome and go together, if that's okay?''

Kate frowned. ''You're asking me out?''

Rafe raked his fingers through his hair and made the wavy strands appear untidily casual. His jaw was very tight. ''Sort of, I suppose.''

''You suppose?'' She didn't want to argue with him, but she couldn't help herself. She'd just about had enough of all this.

''Look,'' he said between clenched teeth. ''The family has a ghost ride and you're invited, okay? That's all I'm saying. If you don't want to go, you don't have to.''

But she did want to go on a Halloween Ghost Ride. She'd never been on one. ''Thanks. I'll look forward to it.''

On Friday, Kate wore a pair of old jeans with a thick pale blue fleece top over a black cotton turtleneck. She slipped her feet into old sneakers. She certainly didn't look like the glamorous woman who had accompanied Rafe to Louise Maxwell's party. But she would have to do. She couldn't dress up for a hay ride into a haunted valley.

Rafe honked the horn of the Jeep outside the house, and she joined him in the front seat. Marc and Crystal were in the back.

Marc made ghostly sounds as she settled her seatbelt around her hips.

"I won't be frightened," she said, glancing over her shoulder, laughing. She was all ready to act as if she didn't have a care in the world.

Crystal chuckled. "Then you've never been on one of Sam's ghost rides. I'll be cuddled up with Marc the entire time."

Kate gave Rafe a sideways glance. He was also wearing his old sneakers, jeans and a thick fleece sweater and turtleneck. All were black, and he appeared foreboding. She certainly wouldn't be cuddling up with Rafe.

The farm gate was decorated with black and orange Halloween symbols of half moons and witches. Lights and wisps of white ghosts were strung into the trees. Sam's mother, Mary, and father, Don, whose brother was John Colson, Rafe's dad, had a hot dog barbecue and steaming cider set up outside the house.

Kate met Sam's brothers, Mike and Lorne. The two men helped them get up on top of a big hay wagon. Kate sat down on the straw beside Rafe, who kept his long legs folded, his hands on his knees. Marc and Crystal kissed and cuddled. Kate glanced away. Oh, she wished things were different. She really had no idea why Rafe had invited her along tonight, other than that Sam had requested her presence, and he probably felt he shouldn't leave her out as she'd had everyone to her party.

"How's the puppy?" Sam asked, sitting down beside Kate.

"His name is Fitz, and he's growing bigger every day."

"You're enjoying him?"

"I love him. And he gets on famously with the cats."

Sam reached across Kate to give Rafe a jab in the leg. "What's with you? You're quiet."

Rafe smiled. "It's going to get noisier, isn't it?"

"Don't give everything away, Rafe. No. It's a perfectly nice, ordinary ride."

"Sure it is, Sam," he teased.

Lorne was driving the wagon, and it took off with a lurch that made everyone fall into one another. Kate landed against Rafe and looked into his eyes. He glanced away and positioned himself a good half foot from her. What had she done to deserve this cold treatment? She tried to think back to before Talisman's last race. Granted, they'd had a bit of a disagreement over whether the horse was ever going to win or not, but surely that wouldn't disturb Rafe that much. He was used to the ups and downs of horse racing.

Looming above them was a huge King Kong model swinging from the branches of an overhanging tree. Everyone began to scream, including Kate, although she wasn't sure why. She knew the model was fake, as were all the ghosts, roaring animals and the strange men popping up with knives and chain saws. Even when the wagon squeezed between a tunnel of haystacks, with blood dripping down the sides of the stacks and hands sticking out accompanied by squeals and cries of help, she knew it was fake. But even so, Kate's heart hammered and her throat was dry with fright. She noticed that Crystal wasn't even looking; she was completely enfolded in Marc's arms. Only Sam, who was alone, and had helped prepare the fright night, was laughing.

"I suppose when you know the source of the trickery, it's not so scary," Kate whispered.

"That's true. But my heart's thumping even so. And this is only the beginning."

Kate began to wish the ride was over. But the wagon entered a tunnel. It was pitch black and very silent, except for the hollow rattle of the wheels and the nervous breathing of the people. Kate could hear the horses hooves on the floor and figured it was probably an old barn they were going through as she was now familiar with hoof sounds on concrete. But when the blood-curdling screams began, and they couldn't see anything, she truly got scared. She began to tremble and moved closer to Rafe. His arm slid around her shoulders.

"It's okay," he said softly in her ear. "It's all theatrical."

"I know, but . . ." The screams grew even more piercing, and he dragged her closer to him, and she clung to him, shaking. And then Rafe was lifting her head, and his mouth covered hers, hot, needy, passionate, the way she had longed for him to kiss her over these past weeks. Only right now the screaming around their heads resembled the pain in Kate's heart.

When the screams ceased, and she rested her head against Rafe's shoulder, she could feel his heart racing. His racing heart, she thought, touching him through his fleece sweater. And my racing heart, she thought. We both have racing hearts now.

As they once more came into the fresh air and began the last trek back to the farm through a lot less frightening landscape, she began to relax slightly, until the wagon tipped and they tumbled off screaming into a hay pile.

Rafe rolled on top of her. "Kate, are you okay?"

She could barely breath with him upon her and the scare of being tipped. "Was that done on purpose?"

"Yes. It's the way they usually end their

wagon rides. Come on. Up.'' He stumbled to his feet and took hold of her hands, drawing her upright.

Kate's legs were trembling as she took Rafe's hands, and he helped her down onto the flat grass. Kate wasn't sure if she dared look at him. What if the kiss had been of the moment, as Rafe's kisses seemed to be. One to seal the deal, one to comfort, one as goodnight for a party. Now one to ease her fear.

''Hot dogs over here,'' Marc said. ''Come and get something before they all go.''

Kate walked ahead of Rafe with Marc and Crystal. She still didn't want to look at him. She didn't want to raise any of her hopes.

At least it was dark, she thought as she sat on a hay bale with Marc and Crystal and ate the hot dogs and drank the piping hot cider. She didn't want to face Rafe in daylight. Besides, he was talking to his cousins and looking as if he were having a good time. He'd obviously taken advantage of the moment with Kate, as he always seemed to. She had to remind herself that whatever she might have learned, however much she felt as if she were immersed in the racing business with the farm, she hadn't been born a horsewoman. That mattered most with Rafe.

By the time they bundled back into Rafe's

Jeep, it was almost midnight. Rafe drove Crystal and Marc into Ellis Corners to their respective homes. Kate looked out of the window to see the home that Marc lived in, which was an apartment above the garage of his parents' house. For some reason Kate had expected Rafe to come from a smaller, older home. This big two-story house was situated on a pretty lot with wide green lawns.

"Nice house," she said as he began the drive back to their farm. "Were you brought up here?"

"My father had it built when I was about ten. We lived downtown before then."

"It's very attractive. Big."

"It's a good size for bringing up a family, like my parents had to."

"Yes," Kate said, wondering if she would ever get the chance to bring up a family, or if Rafe was thinking now of the family he could raise with Rachel.

She sighed and watched the headlights pick out all the twists and turns in the road, and the shapes of hedges and trees. "Rafe, it was fun tonight. Thank you."

"You didn't mind being scared out of your wits?"

"No, not really. It was only fake." It was all fake. Including his kiss?

"That's true. It was fake. But it did seem pretty real at times."

She turned to look at him. "At times," she said softly, wondering if she had the nerve to ask him about the kiss. *Was it real, Rafe?*

They arrived outside the gates and opened them with the wonderful handy-dandy automatic device. They drove through smoothly, and the gates closed behind them. As Rafe drove up to the door, the gravel crunched beneath the tires. Every sound seemed to grate on Kate's nerves now.

"All right?" he asked when he had turned off the engine.

"I had a lovely time," she said. "Great."

Then she climbed from the Jeep and ran to the front door. Her key wouldn't go in properly at first and she could feel Rafe watching her, probably thinking what a klutz she was. She had been a fool from the word go, with her flat tire and her non-horse knowledge. And then to end up falling in love with him. Super fool.

"Can't you open that?"

From behind, Rafe placed his arms around her and took hold of the key. He pulled the key from the lock, reversed it and inserted it back into the lock. "You had it upside down."

She cringed in the circle of his warm arms. "That's how I am to you, isn't it, Rafe—upside down? That's how I've always been. Not quite there for you.''

He still had his arms around her, even though the door had swung inward. Kate could hear Fitz and the cats pattering around inside the house.

''I'm not sure what you are talking about, Kate, but I'll tell you from the moment I set eyes on you, you've always been very much there for me, very much. Now go in, have a good night's sleep, and we'll talk in the morning.''

She turned around in his arms, looked into his eyes and saw his strained features. ''I can't sleep.''

''Oh Kate.'' He closed his arms around her and found her mouth with his in a deep kiss. Keeping her in his arms, he walked her backward through the door. Then he leaned against the door, closing it, holding her. The animals stepped back.

''Oh Rafe,'' she said, and he began to laugh. ''Why you are laughing?''

''You,'' he told her. ''You mix me up so much.''

''Why? I'm pretty straightforward.''

''No. You are *not*. You're complex. You came to me with an inheritance from an uncle you never even knew existed until a few weeks before, and all that baggage about your fiancé. And we're business partners, and it doesn't make sense for us to move into a different relationship.

Besides, I didn't want to rush you. I didn't want to suddenly come on strong and frighten you away. And then it seemed that all you wanted from me was my horse expertise. You only wanted the horse to win. You didn't seem to want me around. Then when Talisman won, all of a sudden you're on top of me. And I realized that I was being used."

"No," Kate protested. "I never used you. But *your* main focus was the horse right from the beginning. You didn't want anything to interfere. Like my party."

"I admit that," he told her. "I just wanted to do my job, prove to you I was a good trainer."

"And you are. I have no doubt about it."

He looked into her eyes. "But you did doubt me for a while there, when Talisman lost those two races?"

"I didn't know what was wrong. You had assured me he was a winner."

"Yeah, I suppose." Rafe smiled. "But he did win the major race we wanted him to win. He's a good horse. At least we got this far with your uncle's dreams."

"At least," Kate said, wondering what this was really all about. When he had made peace with her, was he going to tell her about Rachel? If that was so, why was he holding her so comfortably in his arms as he leaned against the door?

"I've always lived on a wing and a prayer and a gamble," he said. "So here goes, Kate. If we went out and chose a ring together, a beautiful blue stone that matched your eyes, would you consider marrying me?"

She was shocked. Absolutely shocked. "But what about Rachel?"

He frowned. "Rachel?"

"The vet, Rafe. Aren't you just a teeny bit in love with her?"

"If I am, then her husband, Rowan, will be down here like a flash to punch me in the face."

"She's married?"

"She's pregnant. We found out one evening when she was here and almost passed out when she stood up from bending over in the stall. She had to come into the cottage while I got hold of Marc to drive her home."

"But she had lunch with you one day."

"Oh, you're really observant. Yes, she did. Because she doesn't eat when she gets on the job, and Rowan had called and told me to feed her—and the baby. Anyway, Katie darling. This is getting off topic. The babies I want to discuss in the future, will be ours. So will you marry me?"

"On one condition," she told him, cuddling up to him, feeling his arms tighten and loving him even more than she ever expected.

''What's the condition?'' His kisses covered her face, closing in on her mouth.

''That you love me.''

''Oh, I love you. I love you. I love you, Kate. I loved you from the moment I saw your beautiful eyes looking at me through the gate. How about you? Do you love me?''

''Oh, yes, Rafe. I'm crazy about you. I love you so much, so much more . . .''

''Don't mention that jerk's name, but I'm not sure you really loved him after all.''

''I'm not sure either, Rafe. Not now. What I feel for you is so much more.''

''Then let's,'' he said softly, ''put our racing hearts together and really get into a partnership, pardner.''

''I love you,'' Kate whispered, waiting for the kiss that would seal their deal together forever.